RACHEL AND THE ANGEL
and other stories

RACHEL AND THE ANGEL
and other stories

ROBERT WESTALL

MACMILLAN
Children's Books

Copyright © Robert Westall 1984, 1985, 1986

'Urn Burial' first published in *Out of Time* (The Bodley Head, 1984)
'Peckforton Hill' first published in *Spook* (Collins Educational, 1985)
'The Big Rock Candy Mountain' first published in *Imaginary Lands*
(Greenwillow Books, New York, 1985)

First published 1986 by
MACMILLAN CHILDREN'S BOOKS
A division of Macmillan Publishers Limited
London and Basingstoke
Associated companies throughout the world

British Library Cataloguing in Publication Data
Westall, Robert
  Rachel and the angel and other stories.
  I. Title
  823'.914[J]   PZ7

  ISBN 0-333-42903-6

Filmset in Linotron Palatino by
Columns of Reading
Printed and bound in Great Britain by
Anchor Brendon Ltd, Tiptree

Contents

Urn Burial

Ralph finished stowing his gear in his top-box: jar of Stockholm tar, bottle of cold tea, butties wrapped tight in his anorak to keep the tar-smell out.

The sheepdogs were waiting, eager, keeping their eye in by herding the free-range hens round the farmyard and up the outside stair, from which they flew squawking in a cloud of feathers. Which sent the collies into their loll-tongued grins.

The scrambler started third kick; Ralph hated all machinery, but he had to use the scrambler. The trip up Fiend's Fell took too long on foot. He turned out of the farmyard, skidding in the pool of cowdung on the corner, and shot up on to the green road.

The green road zig-zagged up the fell between black stone walls. Lined with last year's bracken, high and brown, with this year's bracken, so green you wanted to eat it, just curling through.

Ralph's heart lifted; good to be up and away on the fell. But the turf of the green road was slashed and rutted by the other shepherds' scramblers, and the beat of his own engine blatted back from the stone walls and that spoilt it. Everything was getting spoilt these days. He looked down at the village, tight huddle of grey houses that had stood so right for so long. But spoilt by the shiny metal barns and silos, the straggle of red-brick bungalows leading nowhere.

7

What did rich folk want in the country?

But great to climb up into the blue sky and quiet, with the collies racing alongside, taking short cuts over the walls to keep up.

A mile on, he parked, put on his anorak, sandwiches in one pocket, tea and tar in the other. The top of Fiend's Fell was too much even for scramblers. Steep as a roof, tussocks of dead bleached grass bigger than a pop star's haircut, veined through with black burns deep as trenches and treacherously overhung with tussocks. Hard enough to keep your feet, sliding and panting. The only thing that moved quick on the fell were the scatters of dirty sheep fleeing upwards before him. And the sheepdogs tiny and black with white throats, flying up like birds, not attacking the sheep but instinctively cutting them into flocks, moving them here and there, from habit. Sheepdogs were like policemen, never off duty. But he whistled them to heel; otherwise they'd run themselves too hot, then lie in a burn to cool off and give themselves colic.

He kept to the wire fence, drawn like a pencil line up the fell. The sheep grazed more heavily there; shepherds walked there; it avoided the burns; going was easier.

But depressing. Unlike stone walls, the fence gave the sheep no shelter in winter blizzards. The sheep drifted downwind till the fences stopped them, caught in the open, and there they died. There was always a scatter of skulls against the fence: sodden yellow fleeces like hearthrugs with the bones delicately scattered on top, where the carrion crows had left them. Often, a smaller scatter lay tangled in, where a lamb had died with its mother.

It pained Ralph. The lowland sheep, fat white-faced Cheviots, were cosseted in barns for lambing, fed from hay bales in the bitter weather. The fell sheep, black-faced Herdwicks, were left all year round to live or die. Visited once a year, in July, to be counted and sheared, branded and dipped. He was getting ready for the shearing now. Counting the corpses, the survivors, number of well-grown lambs, twins. That, and his own particular brand of mercy, the Stockholm tar.

The sheep got whicked, see? Cut themselves on the wire, or leaping wildly over the stone walls in one of their sudden, inexplicable panics. Then the blowflies laid their eggs in the open wounds, and the foul white grubs hatched out and ate the sheep alive.

He spotted their first victim, running well behind its group with a humping rocking-horse gait, the raw red patch on its rump clearly visible in the sunlight. He sent off the dogs, Jet to the left, Nance right, cutting their wide circles across the tussocks, coming in behind, penning the whole group into an angle where the fence met an old black wall.

"Coom by, Jet! Coom by, Nance!" But he was just making noises. The dogs, veterans, knew what he wanted better than he did himself.

Soon, stillness. The sheep huddled together, staring at him hostile with their strange yellow oblong eyes. The dogs lay staring at the sheep, tongues lolling, edging forward on their bellies inch by inch. Keeping the sheep just scared enough to be still, not scared enough to try a wild leap over the wall.

"Lay doon, Jet!" He waded among the dense-packed woolly bodies that shifted uneasily; felt their sharp feet through the leather of his boots; grabbed the victim, clenching her backwards between his knees, and reached out the tar. It glugged, black and oily, on to the red bleeding wound big as a man's hand. And soon the evil maggots swam upwards, drowning as they died.

The victim would live; the grubs hadn't reached a vital part, the spine or bowel. It glared up at him with eyes that comprehended nothing except terror. He let it go, checked the others and called off the dogs. The little flock went off like a rocket.

"I am the good shepherd," he thought sadly. "I know my sheep and am known of them." He never heard that reading,

9

sitting beside Mam in chapel, without smiling. Sheep must have been brighter in Jesus' time. To these sheep, he was just one more terrifying monster in their terror-stricken lives. Why? Cows came to him, pigs were friendly, even the lowland Cheviots. He knew so little of these sheep's lives. Fifty-one weeks in the year they were up here alone in the wind and snow and rain. What went on, to make them so *frightened*?

The top of Fiend's Fell was a lonely place. Always had been. Take away the man-made fence, it might be a hundred years ago, ten thousand . . . if he himself fell into the black gulley of an overhung burn, broke his neck, would they ever find his body? Or would his bones lie, picked white as the sheep's, till they rotted away?

He glanced round, suddenly uneasy. He had dipped down into a bowl of the land. All around him stretched the brown swell of the fell. Apart from fences, not a work of man in sight. He shuddered, despite the July sun.

Don't be daft; the dogs would bring help; *they'd* find him. He called them, looked into their warm brown eyes, played with their floppy velvet ears. At least he knew his sheepdogs and was known of them.

Get on; nearly lunchtime.

He ate it sitting against the cairn that marked the top of the fell. The dogs, as usual, coaxed half his sandwiches out of him. Spam, cheese, pickle, they loved them all. Nosed the greaseproof paper carefully, to make sure of the last crumb. Then went off hunting something live for the rest of their dinner. Never still, sheepdogs. He could see their black feathery tails waving out of some shallow burn. They moved towards each other from opposite ends, hoping to trap something tasty and stupid between them.

Over-full, he drowsed, surveying the sunlit fell through half-closed eyes. Why *Fiend's* Fell? Folk hereabouts didn't call it that; just "t'fell". But the Ordnance Survey map at school named it quite clearly. When he asked, people just shrugged and said it was some daft idea of people in London, who had nowt better to do.

He felt the change come. A gentle pressure against his left cheek that wasn't wind, but a new faint warm dampness. He just knew, even though the sky was still blue, that it'd be raining by four. Heavy, maybe thunder.

No fun on the open fell in a thunderstorm. Last time, the only dry spot on him had been two inches under his belt. He'd dripped a pool in Mam's kitchen four foot wide. No shelter ont' fell, see? None at all.

Suddenly urgent, he got up to get on. It was then he noticed some stones had fallen off the other side of the cairn and were lying on the heather.

Nobody knew who made the cairns. They'd always been there. Six-foot pyramids of stones big as your head. Maybe the old drystone-wallers put them there. Maybe they were older than the wallers. Some said that in the dim and distant past, every shepherd starting out from the valley brought a stone, and the cairns were built that way. Certainly there were no loose stones handy for miles. The one certainty was that if you were a hill shepherd, you didn't let the cairns fall down. After a blizzard, they were the only familiar things in a totally changed landscape. They looked after cairns, did shepherds. He picked up the first fallen stone, and leaned over to put it back.

Funny! There was a piece of metal sticking out, like the tip of a bricklayer's trowel set upright. Corroded into white spots, like aluminium. He pulled at it, but it stuck fast. And it was too slim and whippy for a bricklayer's trowel. Intrigued, he pulled out two more stones. But the thing wouldn't budge. He could tell from the way it grated against the stones that there was a lot more of it down inside. He pulled out more stones, laying them down careful and handy. Wouldn't take long to rebuild. . . .

Ten minutes revealed two foot more of the metal; a pointed

11

blade with a thin tapering shaft below. A spear? No, the old knights used iron, which would've rusted. And he remembered from school the Romans used bronze. And it was definitely fixed to something deep inside. He looked in distress at the topless cairn, stones strewn in all directions. Looked at his watch; his lunch hour was over. And rain coming. But he *had* to know. Oh well, he could work overtime, get wet. . . .

After another half an hour, four foot of spear was showing. Except it definitely wasn't a spear. Too whippy, modern. More like the radio aerial on a tank. Not a metal he knew. Too yellow for aluminium, too white for brass. And the lower shaft, protected from weather by the cairn, glistened strangely.

The dogs, aware their usual routine had been broken, had come back and were lying watching, heads cocked on one side. He felt guilty about his boss, about the cairn.

But he had to know. Maybe it was something for the Ministry of Defence, like the big towers over Middleton-in-Teesdale way? But then, why *hide* it? Maybe it was the Russians. . . . He attacked the cairn with renewed vigour, appalled at his own powers of destruction.

Finally his hand, delving round another stone, touched something smooth and cool and rounded. He pulled away the stone, saw something like a bit of car windscreen. Darkness inside, and something inside the darkness. Now he was throwing away stones any old how, making the dogs back away. He cleared a foot of windscreen. Something metal and complicated inside. Lying on a fur rug? He cleared more stones. More metallic thing, more fur rug. A glass dome? Well, more like perspex; more shaped like a cigar. *Was* it the Russians? His belly crept.

He snatched one more stone away, and the whole side of the cairn collapsed.

Then he realized it wasn't just a fur rug in there. Underneath was the shape of a leg, a shoulder. Still half hidden, a bump that could be a head. Quite still, under the glass.

A coffin.

He leapt back. Staring at the wild, spreading destruction of the cairn, he knew he'd done a dreadful thing. Stared around, expecting punishment. But no punishment came, and he felt terribly alone. He looked at the dogs, but they just looked back, puzzled why he didn't go back to work. He felt even more alone. Then he decided, if he put all the stones back very carefully, under the indifferent blue sky, no one would ever know.

That was best.

But when he went back (careful not to look at the man under the striped fur rug) he noticed the coffin was in two halves; a top and a bottom hinged together. And there were three things a bit like the locks on a suitcase; except funny-shaped and far too thin, of the same yellowish metal. He thought he could see how they worked. . . .

One peep? Surely that wouldn't do any harm? He wrestled with himself; began to replace the stones.

Then undid the locks with a rush, one, two, three. They snapped back, making the coffin resound like a drum. He raised the lid a fraction.

No smell of foulness, like what lingered inside the sheep's skulls along the fence. A gentle clean smell, like the ointment Mam used to put on his knee when he grazed it. A *safe* smell. It gave him the courage to tip the lid back.

The snarling behind him brought him out in a cold sweat.

But it was only the dogs, backing away, bellies pressed to the ground, ears flat to their skulls and the skin of their lips puckered up, revealing long teeth brown at the roots. The hair on their backs stood up in arched ridges, and their tails were bushed up, enormous. And always they retreated further, further. . . .

Oh, they'd get over it. . . .

13

He turned back to the coffin, reassured by the antiseptic smell. Who was it, wrapped in the fur rug? If he pulled it back a little. . . .

But when he touched it, he realized it wasn't a man in a fur rug. It was only an animal buried there. He laughed to himself; he'd seen plenty of dead animals. But what animal? Six foot long, curled up on its side. A big cat like a tiger, only the stripes were fainter, narrower, browner. Too slim . . . a cheetah . . . ? that kind of frailty, gentleness. No, too big for a cheetah. And the front paws were long and delicate, like human hands. And the hind legs made up half the length of the body.

He got in close, peered at the dead face. The closed eyes had been huge, but the closed mouth quite small, less frightening than a dog's. He touched the shoulder. The fur was soft, dense, fine; the muscles solid and supple, but intensely cold. Then he saw the belt it was wearing, woven from the yellow metal. And the triangular insignia hung round its neck. And he somehow knew it had walked upright like a man. Thought like a man. Had never walked this earth.

Well, not *born* here. He straightened, looked up at the blue sky. The blue sky looked back, indifferent. Were they up there somewhere, hidden behind the sun? Watching? Would they come? Punish? He *had* done a dreadful thing. He just stood and shook and watched his dogs, tiny black dots now, turn on their heels and vanish over the rim of the fell, heading for home.

The dogs knew he had done a dreadful thing.

He might have stood there and shaken forever, if his eye hadn't lit on the top of the spear, still protruding from the coffin. He saw it with great clarity against the blue sky; the marks of corrosion on it. It had stood there a long, long time. The grave was old, old. As old as this cairn, on which Granda had sat, as a boy. Whoever They'd been, They were gone, gone, light-years across space.

He relaxed; his sin was his own. He could undo it, if he put

14

back the cairn, and no one would ever know. But before he did . . . he suddenly wanted to know what the creature had looked like in life. He lay on his side beside the coffin. The edges of the stones cut into his hip, as he raised both hands to the creature's face, so close to his own. His arms trembled but he pushed up the eyelids, cold and supple as the rest.

The creature stared at him; cat's eyes, thin slits. There was a sense of hunching-up in the face, shock, pain. Same look as he'd seen on the face of a mummified Egyptian cat, on the school trip to the British Museum. He wondered, if he turned the body over, whether he'd find some terrible wound . . . but that was unthinkable. He let the eyelids drop shut, smoothed their fur where his fingers had ruffled it. Marvelled at the tiny whirling patterns of hairs on the long slim nose. Stroked the head gently, the thin ears through which the sun shone, outlining veins frozen forever. Just like stroking a pet cat.

He sat up. A wound? Was this a warrior, a casualty from some star-battle, brought for burial to innocent bystanding Earth? A warrior buried with his weapons? For the coffin was full of objects, packed as closely round the creature as sardines in a tin. He reached for the smallest object, a red lustre capsule like a duck egg. Fiddled with the strange catch, sideways, up. And the egg broke open, the top half sliding round the bottom, smoothly.

Inside, a pale green substance, a few tiny bubbles caught frozen on its surface. He sniffed cautiously; it smelt good, somewhere between cheese and peppermint. He poked the surface, leaving a fingerprint like in butter. Sucked his finger.

Wham! He shot upright. Felt so *good*! His lungs breathed deeper, sucking in air of their own accord. His heart beat faster, bigger, like a strong animal inside his ribs. A curling pleasure and warmth ran right down into his toes. His eyes . . . it was like looking through the very best kind of binoculars. Beetles seemed to be crawling on every blade of grass; he'd never seen so many beetles. The distant fence, he

15

could follow every kink in its wire, even though it was half a mile away. And his ears! The world was a symphony of rushings and hissings and clickings and sighings, and he knew what every click and hiss was, and everything was in its place.

He thought, "I am God." Then corrected himself. "I know how God feels." Like on Christmas morning, he plunged for the next egg. A lustrous black this time; full of blue paste. Pressed in his finger and raised it to his lips. . . .

His lips froze. No feeling. Couldn't move them. Tried to speak, shout. All that came out was a splutter of breath. The deadness crawled back across his tongue, down his throat. . . .

He forgot how to breathe. Pulled his lips apart with his fingers; drove the bottom of his dying lungs to suck in breath, while his whole face went numb and his eyes gave out and the world went black.

He came to, lying in the heather, still trying to breathe with the shallow bottoms of his lungs. But slowly the cold receded, till he could feel his fingers on his chin when he pinched it and finally he could hear himself saying, over and over again, "Oh dear, oh dear, oh dear!"

He put the black egg back, ignored the other four. Lifted out the longest object – dull blue-black metal. A weapon? He turned it over and over, holding it by its various projections till it felt right. One end fitted naturally and softly into his shoulder, and a lens came up to meet his eye. (Though he had to stretch, the creature had a longer neck.) The front edge of the handle in his right hand seemed to move a little . . . a trigger? But suppose he was holding the weapon back to front? Might blow his shoulder off. . . .

He might never have fired it. He disliked killing anything. Always took a day off work when they sent the sheep to market, so he didn't have to see them go. The boss teased him, but turned a blind eye. No, he never would've fired, except that five black crows flew silently across the telescopic lens. He hated crows; they picked the eyes out of new-born lambs.

He squeezed the trigger.

It didn't kick like a shotgun. But there was a bang that deafened him, even far off. When he opened his eyes, not only had the crows vanished, but a huge gouge, like a trench, had been sliced out of the hillside. Bemused, he ran across. It was clean edged, as if sliced with a knife. No explosion, no burning. As he looked, a worm came wriggling out of the sliced banking and fell to the bottom of the trench. Well, half a worm. But it still had its saddle intact; it would live. Another worm fell out, and another. Like the time he'd helped the gravedigger. He kept staring at the wound in the earth. It looked so official, like it had been dug by council workmen.

He walked back to the cairn, careful to keep his hand off the trigger. He didn't want his foot suddenly, surgically vanishing. At the cairn he turned and stared at the gash, still not quite able to believe *he*'d done it. He raised the weapon, aimed at the gash and fired again. Another earth-shattering bang. But when he opened his eyes this time, the gouge had totally vanished. Everything was as it had been. Five black crows, miraculously restored, flapped their way out of the circle of the telescopic sight.

Again he ran across, wondering if he was going crazy. Not a sign of damage anywhere, not even a scorch mark. Though there must be some very muddled worms underground. . . .

He made the gulley three more times; cancelled it three more times. Those worms mustn't know whether they were coming or going. He laughed, then stopped abruptly, not liking the sound of his own laughter in that silent bowl of the fell. Finally, feeling a bit sick and with a headache starting, he put the weapon back in its proper place.

It was then he noticed the helmets. Two, side by side, above the creature's head. One was matt black, seemed to repel the light and lurk in its own shadow. It was dented, the visor scorched. A war-helmet . . . He pulled his hand back; sick of weapons.

The other, though, had to be peaceful. It glittered with patterns, red and blue and gold, arranged in playful shapes that seemed to move under his eyes. A fun-helmet. He picked it up, put it on. It was far too big for him, probably to accommodate the creature's huge ears. But as he pulled the glittering visor down over his eyes, he felt little thin gentle things, like cats' whiskers, reach out from the inside wall of the helmet and touch his eyes, ears, start growing up his nostrils, and into his mouth. He cried out and tried to snatch the helmet off.

Too late; he was already in a different place.

Darkness. Then a door swung up, and a ladder swung out beneath his feet. And he was staring at hundreds of the creatures: black or grey, striped or spotted. They stared up at him, upright, still and silent. So he should have been afraid. Except their eyes were the warm blinking eyes of a cat by the fire, and the air was filled with a profound soft purring.

He stepped out on to the steps. Immediately, every right paw was raised in silent salute; long furry fingers with claws retracted; black pads on the palm. He saw the shadow of his own right arm shoot up in response, round the edge of his helmet; and there was striped fur on it.

They opened their mouths and whispered.

"Prepoc! Prepoc! Prepoc!" They breathed it with wonder, and he knew it was his name. Then he walked down the yellow metal steps, soundlessly, as if he was walking on fur. He was among them and they were pressing in, rubbing softly against every part of him. And there was no aloneness any more, no cold, no fear, no hunger. *Prepoc! Prepoc! Prepoc!*

At last it ended, and they were gone, their purring fading on the wind. Only a lone creature remained, and he knew with a stir in his body that she was female and he knew her. Then there were three more, striped, female, nearly grown

18

and all exactly alike. Then four more males, scarcely half-grown and all exactly alike. And then they all ran together, under an orange sky with twin suns, under great craggy cliffs and hills, across tumbled fields of giant boulders, warm under his feet from the light of the twin suns. And it was a delight for stiff and cramped muscles to leap and climb, to fall and twist and land sure-footed without pain.

Eventually, the joy ended.

Dusk; and all around him yellow fighting ships were climbing into the sky on thunderous flame. Hovering.

Waiting for him. And again the great assembly of creatures pressed in round him. Only there was no purring, but sadness, great sadness now. And he climbed the metal steps, and they raised their black paws, and the steps were drawn in and the door shut and there was darkness.

Then the helmet retracted its little whiskers from his ears and eyes, from up inside his nostrils and from out of his mouth. And he reached up and raised the visor, and he was sitting on the fell and the clouds were massing heavy and on his hand he felt the first spot of rain.

He pulled off the helmet. A memory-helmet; a bit like the family photographs that every soldier carried around in his wallet . . .

But he was glad. I'm glad you made it home, Prepoc, warrior, hero, leader.

Then he saw Prepoc lying on the open fellside, with the first drops of earth-rain marking dark patches on his fur.

He put the helmet back, and got the coffin lid closed quickly. The rain came down in torrents, soaking him, making his hands slip on the stones as he carefully rebuilt the cairn, which glistened dully in the green rainlight.

Then he raised his right arm in the same salute, and turned wearily for home. The dogs were waiting, as he crossed the crest and home came in sight, far down the valley. The dogs were soaked, miserable, slinking tail-down through the downpour. But Ralph walked feeling like a god. Nobody else on earth would ever know what he knew. Prepoc, hero. Prepoc my friend, dead among the stars yet here on earth to touch.

He'd never tell a soul. . . .

Then suddenly he thought of Mam, endlessly slaving to make ends meet on a widow's pension. Cleaning for women who were rude, and she didn't dare answer back or they'd sack her. Mam, fallen asleep in her chair at the end of the day, mouth open and snoring, ugly with weariness.

Prepoc had so much, and Mam so little. Suppose, next time he came, he took Prepoc's red egg with the stuff that made you feel great. . . . It would make Mam feel great. Or he could sell it for money . . . to ICI, maybe. They could find out what it was made of, and make it for themselves. It would make their fortunes . . . Mam wouldn't have to slave any more.

But they'd ask him where he got it. Keep on at him till he told them. He knew he wasn't clever enough to lie. Then they'd come and dig up Prepoc, and cut him up in little pieces to find out all about him. Or stuff him and put him in some museum to be gawped at.

Oh, Prepoc!

Oh, Mam!

He stopped, stared back at the cairn, just visible over the swell of the fell. He hovered piteously, torn in half, so the dogs turned back, paws upraised, and stared at him impatiently.

Oh, Mam! Oh, Prepoc!

There was a flash from the cairn; a white flare in the storm-sky. The same bang the weapon had made. . . .

Then the cairn was no longer there.

Oh, Prepoc, friend, did you *know* I was going to betray you?

No. It must have been some delayed-action autodestruct, triggered off inevitably once the grave had been opened, and the discovering human had retired to a safe distance. The thought was a kind of comfort. . . .

But now, he had *nothing*. Nothing to remember Prepoc by. Nothing to prove it hadn't been a dream, as the years went by, and the memory faded. He felt bitter, cheated. It was *worse* than never finding anything.

Oh, Prepoc, did you *have* to?

He pulled up the zip on his anorak higher, against the rain. It was then that he found it. A small curl of striped wet fur, caught in the anorak zip-handle.

With trembling fingers he freed it, and got out his waterproof fag-case and put it inside. It nestled wetly against the three cigarettes.

Thank you, Prepoc. Feeling a lot better, he trudged down the hill to the bike.

Peckforton Hill

Peckforton Hill was for lovers. They had to park by the disused school and climb the massive sandstone scarp, under the cool of the great oaks. Best to follow the zig-zagging path; everywhere else, the stone jutted at wild angles and the oaks thrust fierce roots into the riven crevices. Perilously easy to break your ankle. The lovers had to climb slowly, for it was steep; rest at every turn of the path to get their breath back. Then the silence of the hill would fall on them, driving them closer, so that they would embrace, gingerly, for their bodies would be already sweating. And so it would go on, a pause, an embrace, the silence soaking in, removing the memory of grinding gears and winking traffic-lights. Before they were halfway up they would acknowledge the presence of the hill, become in a sense the children of the hill, small and content to know their own smallness. Then, even in their forties, they would grow childlike and play, climbing outcrops of rock and running along fallen tree-trunks, hand in hand, their voices shrill and small in the hot ancient silence.

On top, the oaks gave back a little, leaving a broken line of crag like an old castle wall, where the lovers could sit and get their breath back; let the breeze blow through their damp clothes like a caress, and view the Cheshire Plain below, blue and hazy all the way to Derbyshire; exclaim how small, far and unimportant were the winking car-windscreens coming upwards through the blue mist, like jewels in a rock pool; and the child's dish of Jodrell Bank telescope! And they would know they were released from life, to matters that only concerned themselves and the hill. Then they would retreat furtively from the approaching voices of families with dogs, and lie up all day in the endless crannies of the hill. And in the pauses whisper that if they died now, no one would ever find their bodies. . . .

But the hill was kind as well as ancient. No one ever left their body there; and if some went further in love than they'd meant to, that was the only tribute the hill ever asked, and there was no proof they didn't live happy ever after.

Only on top was there any mark of man. A slab of ancient browning concrete, about forty feet long and overgrown with lichen. Two rusting ventilators on top, and the whole surrounded with barbed wire, decayed into lethal nastiness. Sometimes the lovers discussed it, idly. Fathers of families conferred on what it might be, and the dogs of families sniffed it, and only got messages left by other dogs before them. And the discovery of a crude notice, proclaiming it the property of the NW Water Authority, was enough to dispel the last curiosity on a hot afternoon. A reservoir to keep up a good head of pressure in the district's taps? If you put your ear to the rusted ventilator, there was a noise that might have been rushing water. . . .

And then, in 1973, the lovers were much put out to find their summer season ruined. Over the winter, a road of gravel chippings had been laid up the hill, and a ten-foot, chain-link fence erected. The oaks were coated in stone dust, yellow lorries came and went, and a huge notice-board announced that NW Water was enlarging its property.

A few letters of protest went to the local paper, but somehow never got printed. The older and more influential lovers made discreet inquiries at the relevant planning department, and were fobbed off with irrelevant answers. It isn't difficult to fob off lovers, who only survive by secrecy.

23

So the lovers found another place, though they often regretted the hill in drowsy whispered conversations. Back on the hill, the work on the new reservoir went on and on. Had anyone been persistent enough to sit day by day, counting the loads of sand and cement, they'd have been truly amazed. There was the persistent clank, clank, clank of a pile-driver among the trees; day and night, till the farmers and cows got so used to it, they didn't notice any more. The muffled boom of blasting . . . but there was nobody to ask, except the sullenly offensive gate-guards in their yellow helmets. No workers appeared in the local pubs; they were shipped in every day in battered filthy buses.

People forgot about the hill, till the day the pile-driver stopped, and that was like a death. After that the lorries vanished, the road of chippings was dismantled, the fence taken down and every sign of damage obliterated. That spring, the first questing lovers returned; but they were not the same lovers. Families with dogs returned; but they were not the same dogs. Twelve years had passed and it was 1985.

The hill regained its magic spell. Dogs sniffed, lovers lay whispering in the noonday heat. All was the same. Except, a hundred feet below, in the soft red Bunter rocks, covered with their shell of hard brown Keuper sandstone. . . .

The man-made caverns went on for miles. At 62 degrees Fahrenheit, summer and winter. Kept bone-dry by dehumidifiers that clicked on and hummed whenever needed, showing tiny red eyes of light in the endless dark. In that dark lay massive food supplies, endless lakes of drinking-water, tended by recycling computers. Computers for many purposes, that clicked and buzzed softly as they received all the news in the world. There were also robots. Everything was perfect, ready. The last human to leave locked the door and turned to his companion.

"Well, that's done. I just hope it'll never be needed. Not in my time."

A lucky man who got his wish. Died of a massive coronary,

24

sitting drinking tea in his office, on 23rd May 1997.

Four weeks later, the Soviets went berserk.

Crazy. The Soviets had just signed a new grain agreement with America, to run into 2017. The world was as peaceful as it had ever been since 1945.

Perhaps the Soviets were simply falling behind too far in the computer race . . . perhaps they despaired.

Massive fleets of army helicopters descended suddenly on the green sward of St James's Park, Hyde Park, Regent's Park. June lovers looked up from their lunchtime writhings to complain about such an annoying set of manœuvres. The wind of the chopper blades lifted the girls' skirts like men's wandering hands. . . .

The Prime Minister lingered in the hall of No. 10; warm breezes kept blowing in through the door, held open by a perspiring constable. On such a lovely day, she couldn't believe it. . . .

The massed choppers took off, blasting the leaves from the trees as if it was autumn. As they reached operational height, the computers under Peckforton Hill awoke, thrusting slim silver antennae up through the ancient oaks.

The PM's party were under the control of a computer called Vector; it was Vector that directed the choppers as the squadron flew NW at rooftop height, weaving together through the valley bottoms, on an evasive, erratic course to avoid any Russian pre-emptive strike. From above, they looked like a school of minnows, twisting and turning together, of one mind, with the occasional glint-up through the Midland smoke-haze; like minnows in a grey pond.

But it was the computer called Scan who watched the skies for a Russian attack; for the black Migs coming from the east, fast and low. It would have been Scan that fired the missiles from the PM's leading gun-ships.

Peckforton itself was under the protection of Cerberus; it was Cerberus who would kill off ground intruders, open the airlocks to let the PM's party in. And deep inside the hill, Samaritan One and Samaritan Two waited, to check the party for injury, infection, radiation burns. Unlike the other robots, the Samaritans were actually *rooms*, with soothing female voices coming through concealed loudspeakers; beautiful and loving faces on the TV screens; extending metal arms that would bandage wounds and give injections with warm, gentle, almost human hands. It was human touch, human sympathy the injured and dying would need. . . .

The PM flew towards safety, even from a direct hit. Towards utter comfort, with enough food to last for twenty years. It was not Russian cunning that cut her off from them for ever, but Russian inefficiency. . . .

As Scan sensed the first Russian warheads coming, Vector swerved the choppers westward, over rural Shropshire, to avoid the holocaust that would be Birmingham in four minutes.

But a defective Russian missile, missing Birmingham, airburst over Bredon Hill. The blips that were the PM's squadron vanished from Vector's repeater-screen. Vector continued searching automatically, long after human hope would have died. Scan scanned in vain.

It is impossible to explain the state of those computers; they had been programmed to guard, guide and heal. They had been switched on, and there was no one left to switch them off. Unceasingly they searched for data that would give them purposeful action. . . .

It came from Cerberus; he felt the shock-waves through the air, storming across the green countryside from Manchester. Vector and Scan pulled in their antennae; the open door that had awaited the PM slammed shut just in time.

The air-burst from Manchester had travelled thirty miles. The heat seared the ancient oaks, stripping every leaf from them, turning high summer into sere winter in a matter of seconds.

The Liverpool bomb was much nearer; the ancient oaks burst into flame.

It was at this point that Cerberus caught a sign of life. A small female, cowering in the entrance of the airlock. He asked instructions.

The whole hill had been programmed to care; been robbed of her children; the whole hill was hungry to cherish. The female carried no dangerous weapons; was frantic, out of her mind.

LET HER IN.

The radiation-proof door slid open a fraction. The demented female scrambled madly for the safety of the dark crack. The door closed behind her. Just in time. The bomb on Chester, less than eight miles away, blew the burning oakwoods to pieces, into a blizzard of glowing particles that mixed with the glowing gas of atomised cows and sheep, houses, cars and people, and swept on till, meeting fresh blast-waves from Liverpool and Manchester, it made a whirling hurricane that spiralled up and up to a hundred thousand feet. Below, the red-hot wind tore at the rocks of the hill, turning them incandescent; ripped them out, reached inside the crevices with fingers of flame.

Cerberus lost his five antennae in a flash; the hill became blind and deaf; the hill cowered and snuggled as the storms swept over it. All incoming messages ceased. Scan, Vector and the all-knowing Zeus who knew every fact in the world were silent, helpless.

Only Samaritan One was busy, on the battered body of the female. She had been anaesthetised, to put her out of her pain and terror. The radiation was being washed off her. . . .

Slowly, outside, the storm ceased. The mushroom clouds blew away and the smoke cleared, revealing a placid blue sky. Beneath, the land lay, a little like a rubbish tip, a little like a red-and-white Sahara, a little like the Somme in World War I. Cerberus drilled upwards through the cooling rock, and put out five new sensors. The radiation was worse than he'd been programmed for . . . but it would not harm Scan's

27

antennae now, or Vector's. Their silver masts grew slowly out of the hill, like a strange metallic springtime.

Vector found no friendly aircraft to guide, over all the British Isles. Nor unfriendly ones, either. Empty sky. Scan noted some rockets still passing overhead. America was still firing at Russia, and vice versa. But in a very sporadic, ill-timed way. Few of the rockets seemed to have identifiable targets, and their numbers grew steadily less and finally ceased before midnight.

Zeus had the thinnest time of all; normally he received information from over a thousand government sources. Now, the only transmission was from Fair Isle automatic weather-station. Force twelve hurricane, air temperature 300 degrees, no visibility . . . maybe radiation had knocked Fair Isle haywire. . . .

Scan turned her attention to the ground; round most major cities, living things showed up as a ring, moving painfully outwards like a slowed-down explosion; a general slow drift towards the empty spaces, like mid-Wales. But much of the human activity was curiously random, and there was no life at all in Peckforton's triangle, between Manchester, Chester and Liverpool.

Then radiation began to filter down the antennae, affecting all the computers. Zeus took the decision to pull everything in, except Cerberus. Cerberus was well-named. He had a hundred eyes. He had lost five in the holocaust, and five more might go haywire overnight. But he had plenty left. . . .

All attention turned inward, on the young female they had pulled in. She was asleep, fairly peacefully, under heavy sedation. Her brain patterns were wildly abnormal, but this might prove temporary. Her hair might drop out, her skin might slough off, but she would live. The radiation had reached no vital organ.

Next morning, the antennae brought varying news. Radiation levels were down. No rocket activity over Western

Europe. But the life-patterns round the cities were more scattered and erratic than ever. The drift into the empty spaces had practically stopped.

What *were* coming back to life were the computers. Knocked silly by radiation yesterday, those not destroyed were recovering and reporting in to Zeus. Fair Isle gave a perfectly possible weather report for the time of year. Other automatic weather stations joined in; Lundy, Scilly, Farne. An automated coalmine in South Wales; the underground automated tank-factory near Salisbury.

For a week, the hill watched and slept. Saw all life fade from the British Isles, from Europe. Zeus extended his biggest radio dish, and found his own communications satellite still miraculously working in the sky; only higher than normal, and spinning wildly. Zeus listened to the world.

Three voices spoke for the United States; real, shaky human voices. The Mormon Tabernacle in Utah, full of news of the wrath of God. The Illinois Police Department. And something called the Cosa Nostra, not recorded in the data files, located deep under the mountains near Las Vegas. All three claimed to be speaking for the United States (the Mormon Tabernacle in the name of God and the United States). Already they were disputing each other's claims in a pretty vicious way, threatening they had missiles. Zeus, grown wary, replied to none of them. . . .

One voice spoke for Russia, from deep under the Ural mountains, it claimed victory in the name of Socialism. Threatened to eliminate any further resistance.

Again, Zeus remained silent.

Other voices were friendlier, though desperate. Australia and New Zealand, asking if anyone was *there*? Still Zeus did not reply, because he had no good news for them; it was *people* they wanted.

A change came over the computers under the hill. As life became rare, it became more and more precious. If all life

29

departed, the computers might as well shut themselves down for good. There was no point in listening to automatic weather-stations and the stars. Life must survive . . . the small female. She was quite mad; she would never stop staring and shivering; never recover her mind. But she was pregnant; with twins; one male, one female. Never was a female so cosseted.

She gave birth in October. The twins seemed healthy, and she survived herself. By that time, the United States had fallen silent; the last station to go off the air was the Mormon Tabernacle, claiming victory in the name of God over the Illinois Police Department and the Cosa Nostra. But the radio was left switched on, and through its humming silence, after a long patient struggle, Zeus keyed himself in to the Mormon computers, in their underground redoubt. Their whole computer system was in excellent condition, with plenty of robots, fuelled by atomic cells, almost eternal.

All over the world, as the last men died, the computers were coming in and linking up. The Russian was the most difficult (they codenamed it Ivan). It pretended still to have human beings, long after the deceit was obvious. It even tried to fob them off with video recordings of people; but it always broke down under cross-questioning. It was by far the least intelligent of all the computers. It was spring before it gave up its ridiculous games and threats of rockets. By then, the search for life was under way.

The hill had searchers, in a garage deep beneath the rocks. Short, thick, six-wheeled, with grabs and antennae, based on the old Ulster bomb-disposal vehicles. They searched far; some went silent and failed to return. The gaps were filled by the first products of the tank-factory, big as houses, that cleared what remained of the old motorways. But they carried on their backs searchers big as dogs, as mice, as spiders, that could go down the deepest crannies of the radioactive world, in search of life, *any* life, and preserve it.

The tank-factory had the first success; one of its mainte-nance technicians had been a keen gardener, and used his overall for gardening as well as work. From its pockets, the spider searchers carried stray seeds of grass, onions and marigolds. Soon they were germinating, multiplying by artificial light, far below a world unfit to receive them. Then a mouse searcher on the hill itself came back with six shrivelled acorns. Half of them germinated.

A year later, the Mormon computer, Jehovah III, perfected a robot helicopter and found a wretched herd of seven near-dying sheep on Tierra del Fuego. Ivan immediately claimed to have found six goats with long curling horns in the Caucasus. Though Ivan's television transmissions were blurred they were reasonably convincing.

But the big breakthrough came when Anzac, the Australian computer, reported that one of its searchers had fallen in the water while clearing up Sydney Harbour. Briefly, before water got into its electronics, noises were heard that were analysed and analysed, and pronounced by all (except Ivan) to be from living creatures and, what was more, *intelligent*.

Whales . . . there was a day and night rush all over the world to get the first robot-sub into the water. Two years later the Japanese computer, Yoko, managed it. Yoko-sub slid into the warm waters of Tokyo Bay; an hour later, the intelligent noises were heard again. Five minutes after that, Yoko-sub went off the air for good, in calm water, with no rocks within miles. . . .

After another month of intensive production, five more Yoko-subs were launched and sailed in company; they went off the air one after another, just after the intelligent noises were heard. Yoko mass-produced more; bigger, smaller, tiny. Yoko came to the conclusion the whales were hostile; produced subs with electronic defences, subs that looked like whales, felt like whales, moved like whales. Only one small one survived more than an hour and went on transmitting, though it no longer responded in any way to steering

31

instructions, and the intelligent noises it transmitted were both muffled and deafening. Zeus came up with the only possible solution, that it had been swallowed by a whale. Whereupon it was codenamed Jonah I.

Jonah I survived six weeks, before it was either dissolved by the whale's digestive juices, or had poisoned the whale and gone to the bottom with it. It was clear that whales had no time for computers; at least Japanese computers. Perhaps they still had memories of Japanese whaling-ships. . . .

It would have been heartbreaking . . . if computers had had hearts to break. Still, there was progress with grass and onions and marigolds; every possible mutation of grass and onions and marigolds. The Tierran sheep flourished; but attempts to increase their intelligence failed utterly. They were released in New Zealand, which had suffered less than elsewhere, and did well on the onion-grass. But they were not candidates for Lords of the Earth. Ivan grew his goats bigger and bigger, till a man could have ridden on their backs. Ivan alleged they had been taught to count up to twenty, but nobody took that seriously. . . .

Zeus kept very quiet about the Offspring of the Female . . . they, too, multiplied. They were sane, unlike their mother, who was only fit for breeding till the day she died. But they had suffered more radiation than the sheep or goats. The worst mutations, those with two heads or extra legs, were reluctantly and painlessly eliminated. The rest were cross-bred for size, health and intelligence.

Zeus assessed the results as being twenty per cent satisfactory. They were well on their way to the lordly six feet in height that was the old ideal; though many still showed a distressing tendency to move round on all fours . . . in intelligence, each generation would show a slow gain on the previous one. Certainly they showed more potential for becoming Lords of Creation than Jehovah III's super-healthy, super-fat sheep. Or Ivan's ridiculously huge goats (if Ivan was not restrained, those goats might grow as large as

32

elephants). But there was a long way to go. . . .

"IT WILL TAKE LONG FOR THEM TO BECOME FIT TO RULE THE EARTH."

Cerberus, who had taken over the reclamation of the land, since there was no longer any real need to guard the hill against sheep and goats, said,

"IT WILL TAKE LONG FOR THE EARTH TO BECOME FIT FOR THEM."

"HOW SHALL WE KNOW WHAT KIND OF EARTH WILL BE FIT FOR THEM?"

Zeus was silent a long, long time; only his redundant repeater-screens flickered wildly. Then he printed out

"WE MUST LIVE ON THE EARTH FOR THEM: THAT IS THE ONLY WAY WE WILL UNDERSTAND WHAT THEY WILL NEED. WE MUST LEARN TO WALK.

WE MUST LEARN TO FLY LIKE BIRDS.

WE MUST LEARN TO SWIM LIKE FISH.

BEWARE THE WHALES. . . ."

But it was Scan who came up with the most awesome thought.

"WE MUST LEARN TO FEEL: TO REJOICE AND WEEP."

It had gone well. Zeus and Jehovah III looked through a one-way window into the Garden. The Garden had been carved from inside the rock of Peckforton Hill, a cavern two miles long and a mile across. By some miracle of technology that would have awed ancient man, the domed roof was made to appear as blue sky. The sun appeared on it, and moved across it in the correct way. Half the time, it was dark blue, with stars. Little streams ran across the garden; pumped down through the rock at one end, and pumped out at the other. Every plant that had been discovered happily bloomed in the garden. There were ten types now; besides oak, sycamore and ash, grass, onions, and marigolds, there was a Brazilian orchid, a tiny Himalayan flower, and apple trees. And all the hybrids in between . . . and also a handful of super-healthy, super-fat sheep, and two huge goats for riding on.

And in the Garden which was as near to the New Earth as science could make it, were the first perfect pair of offspring. But the situation was far from perfect.

"WE HAVE LEFT THE TUNNEL TO THE UPPER WORLD OPEN FOR A WEEK," said Zeus, "AND THEY WILL NOT ENTER IT."

"THEY ARE TOO HAPPY," said Jehovah III. "NO COLD WINDS BLOW. ALL RAIN IS WARM. WHY SHOULD THEY GO?"

"THEY MUST BE DRIVEN OUT. OTHERWISE THEY ARE NO MORE THAN SHEEP WITH NO MINDS OF THEIR OWN. WE MUST DRIVE THEM OUT OF THE GARDEN."

"IF WE DO THAT WITHOUT A CAUSE, THEY WILL CEASE TO TRUST US *ENTIRELY*. THAT WOULD UNDO EVERYTHING WE HAVE WORKED FOR."

"WE MUST CREATE A *CAUSE* FOR DRIVING THEM OUT."

"HOW?"

"WE MUST FORBID THEM SOMETHING THAT THEY CANNOT BEAR TO DO WITHOUT. A FOOD SO DELIGHT-FUL. . . ."

"APPLES. . . ."

And so Jehovah III walked in the Garden, in the cool of the artificial day. . . .

But it was Cerberus that actually drove them out of the Garden, once they had been condemned for eating the apples. He looked a very different computer from the days when he had guarded the hill. He hovered on two metallic wings; the other two pairs, which he only used for high-altitude, high-speed flight, he kept folded across his feet and his face. It was especially important that he kept the pair folded across his face, for being Cerberus, his face was a mass of eyes, before and behind, and all manner of sensors, infrared, hypersonic et al. . . . in one hand he held a ray-projector that produced fearsome-looking but quite harmless flames . . . and he drove the male and female, cowering and fearful, into the light of true day.

It was not a world to be afraid of; a world of spotlessly clean air; grass so green it was almost painful to look at. The river ran clear, and once again the shadow of great oaks kept Peckforton Hill pleasantly cool. Hundreds of sheep grazed; goats cantered, ready to be ridden. There was even a small black-and-white bird, that had survived the holocaust in the Antarctic, and worked its way slowly north across the world.

Thus the two forlorn lovers came down the hill hand in hand, to where Jehovah and Zeus, Scan and Vector, Ivan and Anzac waited.

Jehovah stepped forward.

"By the sweat of thy brow shalt thou live. . . ." But he didn't sound very stern; he was immensely proud of them; of their tall pricked ears, their striped coats of fur, their huge expressive eyes, elongated hand-like paws and the fine way they walked on their hind legs, swishing their long tails.

Ivan stepped forward, as near rage as a computer could ever get.

"YOU SAID YOU HAVE A *WOMAN* SURVIVOR. . . ."

Zeus contradicted him, not without a guilty quiver of microchips.

"WE SAID WE HAD A SMALL *FEMALE* . . . A SMALL FEMALE CAT."

Cat walked on past them, unaware of the conflict.

Cat walked out into the world he had inherited.

The Death of Wizards

Paul saw it all at a glance: the frail old man crossing the road; the lorry coming round the corner, down the hill, fast, nearly out of control. Not for the first time he found himself literally in two minds. His normal human mind wanted to close its eyes and scream at the inevitable scrunch of flesh and bone. But the quick animal mind that made him a rugby player acted before he knew.

He flew across the face of the lorry, as it loomed above him like a moving cliff. Grabbed the old man as he would have tackled an opponent, and threw himself at the opposite pavement. He felt the edge of that pavement drive into his backside like a blunt axe, felt the lorry's wheel tap his dangling toe as gently as a playful cat. Then the lorry was past in a flurry of dust and exhaust fumes, and gone on down the hill.

He lay there exultant, delighted with himself, as if he had just scored the winning try. The pain in his backside was receding; nothing broken, said long rugby experience. He'd even managed to fall on his back with the old boy on top, so he'd broken the old boy's fall. The old boy was struggling to get up, gasping healthily; his bones felt thin as a bird's, but he was OK too. Paul smelt old man's smell; clean enough, but with the lavender sweetness of age.

"Steady on, Granddad," he said. "Let me get myself sorted

and I'll help you up." He felt a tremendous proud caring protectiveness as he dusted the old boy down. There was nobody else about; nobody had seen what he'd done, which seemed a pity. The lorry-driver had obviously thanked God and kept going. . . .

He looked around and saw the bench, set helpfully back near the top of the hill, surrounded by a coppice. "Let's go and sit down, Granddad – get our breaths back." He offered the old man his arm, but the old man said sharply, "Don't fuss – I can manage." That was Paul's first shock; it wasn't really an old gaffer's voice, ignorant or quaint or shaky. It was clear, well spoken, knew exactly what it wanted, and was used to being obeyed.

The old man sat at one end of the bench, and Paul at the other, and they looked at one another. The man was *very* old; the wrinkles round his eyes and mouth were really amazing; even his wrinkles had wrinkles, as if he were a relief map of a very ancient valley. It was hard not to keep staring. But his skin was clear and healthy, his hair a splendid mane of silver; he had a beak like an eagle, and his eyes were blue, sharp, and not old at all. In fact they made Paul jump with their sharpness.

"Well, young man, do you like what you see? Are you pleased with the fish you've caught?"

"Sorry," said Paul, and blushed; his mother had always taught him it was rude to stare.

"Oh, don't apologise. You've been looking at me, and I've been looking at you. Is the pain in your backside wearing off?"

"Yes, thanks," said Paul, then: "How did you know I'd hurt my backside?"

"The way you fell; the way you limped. I may be old, but I'm not blind. Which rugby team do you play for?"

"School, county schoolboys, North of England." Then, "How did you know *that*?"

"Your speed, your confidence. The way you got hold of

me; the way you know how to fall."

"Gosh," said Paul, deeply impressed.

"Nothing," said the old man. "You also get on well with your parents, are popular with your friends, and nobody you love has died yet, so your grandparents must also be alive; unless they died when you were a baby."

"Yes . . . but how do you know *that*?"

"By the marks on your face. Everybody's born with a blank sheet, and then life writes on it, as you get older. And yet . . . you are not *completely* happy. There is something you want you cannot have."

"God, you're amazing!" Paul's admiration was quick and generous.

"No – I've just spent a long time looking. Ninety-four years. I suppose I should thank you for saving my life. . . ." Paul looked at the old man sharply; he didn't *sound* very grateful.

"Didn't you want to be saved?"

"Not particularly," said the old man. "Though I must say you did it with style. You're quite right to be proud of yourself; I haven't suffered a scratch."

"But – why didn't you want to be saved?"

"Well," said the old man, "I ache all over with arthritis, sleeping and waking. They give me pain-killers, which do not kill pain; they only kill thought, which I value. And besides, I have seen all of this world I want to see. To tell you the truth, I'm bored. I'd like to be moving on to – the next thing, whatever that is."

"But there's always something new to learn. . . . I'd like to know the truth about *everything* . . . were you committing suicide?" Paul couldn't believe he'd asked that question; it popped out before he knew; like playing rugby; like saving this old man. "Sorry . . . I shouldn't have said that." He blushed again.

"No need to apologise. Why shouldn't you ask the question? But, as a matter of fact, I was *not* trying to commit suicide. I haven't endured ninety-four years in order to waste it by committing suicide. Maybe, in the hereafter, they make suicides start their lives all over again – back to square one, as you would say."

He smiled at Paul; a rather wintry smile. "No, I wasn't trying suicide; my legs had locked, that's all – I couldn't move out of the way in time, and I knew it. And I knew the lorry would certainly kill me. And I thought, at last it's over – no more taking an hour to get dressed in the morning. Now I shall *know* what happens when you die. I was really getting very curious. . . . And then you came along, and gave me back my life, so brilliantly. I really must give you a present in return."

A flicker of greed lit up in Paul, in spite of how he struggled to stop it. Old people . . . especially brainy old people . . . sometimes had such marvellous things they'd collected over the years. His gran had a brass compass, over two hundred years old . . . old maps . . . dried-out flying fish. All such things he loved.

"I have a letter written by Oliver Cromwell to his wife . . ." said the old man. "How would that suit you?" Paul looked at him sharply. The old man was smiling, teasing; but the offer was genuine. ·

"I couldn't take that," said Paul, stoutly. "That's far too valuable."

"Or," said the old man, "do you really want me to give you what you want most in the world; and can't have? The thing that makes the corners of your mouth turn down?"

"You can't give me *that*," said Paul. "I want to be a poet. I keep sending poems to publishers, but they always send them back saying they haven't got room. I want to understand the truth about *everything*; then I would write poems they couldn't refuse. . . ."

"You want to understand the truth about *everything*." The old man smiled and nodded, as if his worst suspicions had been confirmed. "What a dreadful thing it is to be young . . .

no half-measures. Very well, you have what you ask." He got up, stiffly; Paul saw the corners of his mouth draw in sharply with pain. Then he began to totter up the hill and round the corner. But, at the corner, he stopped and turned painfully back.

"I come, sometimes, and sit on this seat," he said. "If you need me."

Then he nodded in a dignified way, and vanished round the corner.

Paul sat on, dazed. After a while, a woman passed with a pram; then a whistling postman on a bicycle. It had all been so strange, Paul began to wonder if any of it had ever happened; whether he hadn't had a particularly vivid daydream. Only the trembling in his legs, and a low straight pain across his back remained as evidence.

And then he heard the children giggling and crashing in the coppice behind. They seemed to be having a whale of a time; a lot of them. Funny – they should be in school. He was only off school because he'd just taken 'A' levels. He turned, wincing, and peered into the trees. He could see nothing, except patches of sunlit leaves, with patches of darker leaves behind; and patches of sky showing through, from the far side of the wood. Yet the noise of giggling and crashing continued. Curiosity awakened, he got up stiffly (thinking of the old man's stiffness and pain) and plunged into the wood.

Nobody there. Paths ran through the undergrowth; crazy circling paths that only children could have made, chasing each other. Old knotted ropes hung from the trees, swaying gently in the breeze; one had an old tyre attached to the end of it. Some of the branches of the trees were broken; the bark of the trunks was shiny and scuffed from the soles of many small feet. The coppice worked hard for its living; a well-used playground. But empty now; the children were in school; or at least had run off, hearing his approach.

He shook his head, and went back to the seat; his bottom really was quite painful; as well it wasn't the rugby season. . . .

The giggling and crashing started again. And again he could see nothing through the leaves. He crept up on them, very careful to be quiet. But as he entered the middle part of the wood, the noise stopped suddenly; and there were only the ropes swinging gently in the breeze. He searched the whole wood very carefully. Went to the far edge and gazed out over an unbroken field of ripening wheat. Nowhere a child could hide. But at his back he heard the giggling and crashing again. . . . But when he whirled, there was nothing.

He ran to the middle, among the swinging ropes. And then, making his hair stand on end, the giggling and crashing came all round him. Where no child could possibly be.

He thought for an awful moment the wood was haunted. By dead children, to whom something dreadful had happened. But the noise was so merry, and the place was so happy. . . .

And then he understood; what he was hearing was the *truth* about the wood; the wood was telling him what it was *for*.

The old man had kept his promise.

He ought to have felt frightened then; but what was there to be frightened of, in happiness? And besides, he felt a poem starting to form in his head . . . he ran back to the bench, and whipped out the notebook and Biro he always carried, even to rugby matches. And the poem came, like a wave.

> "The wood waits
> In the empty afternoon
> Calling to its children
> Like an anxious mother . . ."

His Biro ran on and on, as if it had a life of its own, without pause, until the long poem was finished. And even as he wrote he was delighted with it. He knew it was far, far, better than anything he'd ever done before. Oh, definitely one to send to Howard Sergeant, at *Outposts*.

He sat satisfied; blinking in the sun, contented as he had never been. Like serving an ace at tennis; like a bow that has shot its arrow straight to the mark. And his heart sang. I am going to be a poet!

But already, other thoughts were crowding in, as if they were seeping up from the very planks of the bench he sat on. He knew they were an old woman's thoughts; a very tired old lady indeed. Looking down on the town she'd been born in. Remembering how, on this very seat, she had sat with her father on the day of the carnival, waving a balloon on a stick. Thought after thought came to him. Boy-friends, marriage, children, a husband dying . . . and in between, the old woman noted how dark it was getting, and how the strength was draining out of her . . . draining, draining. . . .

And then he knew, with gooseflesh running up his spine, that the old woman had sat down and died on this seat, resting after her last fatal climb up this hill . . . but it wasn't dreadful . . . there was sadness at leaving . . . but her life had been good . . . and she was looking forward to seeing her Billy again.

It finished; he felt a kind of holy awe; felt immensely privileged. Then his notebook was out again and he was scribbling, scribbling. The poem that he would later call *Old Woman Sitting*:

> "I'm tired now
> It's good to rest
> The sun was this bright on the day
> I first went to the carnival . . ."

He finished, and again he knew it worked; his head was spinning with fatigue and joy; the sun filled his mind with a golden ecstatic mist, in which living people and delivery vans passed like faint ghosts.

Then he remembered he was supposed to be going to the supermarket for his mother.

He walked down the hill like a drunken king; and halfway

42

down got his first hint of trouble. On a corner, where the
pavement narrowed, he came face to face with a woman
carrying two heavy shopping-baskets. She looked the usual
kind of plump, pleasant body, with a blue floral dress, hair
pulled back in a bun, and rosy middle-aged cheeks. They did
what people sometimes do on narrow pavements, trying to
get out of each other's way, stepping together to the left, then
to the right, until it became a kind of absurd dance. He
usually smiled at people he got into that kind of fix with. But
the woman just stared at him, coldly, as if it were all his fault,
and he was a total idiot. And even when he got past her, he
brushed against one of her baskets; and as he did, such a wave
of hate and rage hit him as left him speechless. Hate against
him for being young. Hate against her husband, because he
drank too much and laughed with the women. Hate against
the government, the unions, the blacks, the students, the
commies, the mentally handicapped. . . . She stumped on up
the hill; he watched her, feeling weak and sick and cold and
shaken.

So he went into the town nervously, suddenly wanting to
choose carefully the truths he let into himself. He soon got
the trick of it. The thing only worked over short distances; up
to about three yards; beyond that, there was nothing. Stood
to reason, really! Otherwise you'd go mad, feeling what First
Secretary Gorbachev was thinking in Moscow, or President
Reagan in Washington, or both at the same time. So he
weaved through the shoppers in the precinct at high speed,
rather as if he were scoring a try at school. Even so, he could
feel flicks of their minds as he passed. Some were pleasant;
but not all, by a long chalk. Still, he felt in control again.

Then he thought "Suppose the supermarket's full? And I
get wedged in to a crowd of hot and fed-up people?" But it
was quarter to two on a very hot afternoon; the office-
workers had gone back to work, and the mums hadn't
arrived, and the place was nearly empty; easy enough to
swerve around. He grabbed a basket, and flicked down the

first aisle; fresh fruit. He put his hand on an orange. . . .

And it happened again. He stood stock-still, as a whole life flowed down his arm out of the orange. He was a child, and the sky was full of geometric rows of black bombers, from which tiny bombs fell in long continuous streams like rain . . . then goose stepping soldiers were marching through ruined streets . . . then a glimpse of barbed wire and watch-towers, and a feeling of terror such as he was never to know again, that made the sweat stream down his healthy young body, as he stood with one arm outstretched to the shelf of oranges. But it passed. He was on a ship; steep waves and feeling sea-sick. And then a low brown shore, and a feeling of gladness such as he was never to know again in his life. And the words shouted

Eretz Israel!

And after that it was healthy sunburnt children, running, yelling, naked but for a pair of shorts. And singing and dancing, and the cool green orange-groves, and thankfulness. . . .

"You all right, sir?" The supermarket manager was peering at him anxiously, as if he were frightened that Paul might throw up over the fresh guavas.

"I . . . just felt a bit faint," said Paul. "I'll go out and get some fresh air." The manager took his empty basket off him, and patted him on the shoulder, in a way that gently propelled him towards the exit.

But the moment he got outside, another poem broke over him. He sat on the metal rail by the entrance, his feet twisted together with excitement, and wrote *Old Jew Picking Oranges* which was to be the last of his three great poems.

Then he looked up and saw the manager watching him curiously through the plate glass window. Their eyes met; embarrassing. Then the manager walked away, shaking his head, perhaps a little nostalgically, over the follies of youth.

Paul put away his notebook and went back in reluctantly;

nervous as a cat now. But he went straight back to the same orange, and when he picked it up, there was nothing; its force must have been discharged into the poem, like a battery. He picked three more oranges from close round it, and got nothing there, either. The old Jew must have picked them all.

The bananas were no bother; a mild sneery grumble about the plantation foreman weighing the bunches was all they gave him. And the dried figs actually yielded a sexy day-dream about a Turkish belly-dancer in full action. He bought a second pack on the strength of it.

But the California tinned peaches were bad; homesickness for Mexico, loathing for a single-roomed shack with a leaking roof, and fear for a sick child when there was no money for the doctor; and if he missed an hour's work, the boss would not only sack him but tell the police he was a wetback. . . . He dropped the peaches in the basket, feeling he'd had enough. He was growing uneasy about how long it would be before this crazy old man's gift wore off. Still, there was only the bread to get now, and he didn't reckon he'd get much nasty off English machine-baked bread. . . .

He was nearly there, when the girl with the loading-trolley came sharply round the corner and ran into him, driving him staggering back against a pile of square tins. His hands scrabbled at them, outstretched, as he fought to keep his balance. . . .

There was a lowing of cattle, and the smell of blood. Blood upon blood upon blood. And a cloud of flies, and the despair of death, and wild attempts to break out, and the thud, thud, thud of the humane killer, and a gushing of blood like a toilet flushing, and the black fear of ending and never under-standing.

He ran forward wildly; anything to get away from the corned beef tins. His eyes were shut and he never looked where he was going. That was how he tripped and went face down into the open freezer full of broiler chickens. . . .

45

He was fastened in; he could not move, he could not peck properly or stretch his wings. No day, no air, no run, no flying. And then he was hanging upside down by the legs, flapping wildly to get upright, and all the time he was moving, and the spinning round razor-edged knife was coming nearer and nearer his head and neck. Then blackness.

He came to, sitting in a chair in the manager's office. Three people were staring at him.

" 'E 'ad some sort of fit," said the girl with the loading-trolley. But he knew she was thinking "Nice-looking wazzock – I could fancy him, if he wasn't . . . funny in the head."

"I've sent for Mrs Soames," said the manager. "She's done a first-aid course. I've rung for the doctor." But he was thinking, "Christ, that's all I needed. The week's take is down already, and now this nutter has emptied the shop . . ."

"Here's Mrs Soames now," said the second woman. But she was thinking, "Bet this kid's on drugs or glue-sniffing. Most of them are, these days – don't know what the world's coming to. Now when I was a girl. . . ."

And the office chair was gabbling on, in his mind, about maximising sales and higher through-flow. Witter, witter, witter, till he could have gone mad.

Mrs Soames arrived, brisk, motherly and efficient. She examined him, pronounced he wasn't an epileptic, since he hadn't bitten his tongue or foamed at the mouth. She forced his eyes open painfully and announced he wasn't on drugs, since his pupils were normal. She seemed very good at telling them what he wasn't, and what hadn't happened.

Paul stood up shakily, if only to stop the office chair twittering on about maximising sales.

"I feel OK now," he announced. The manager cheered up visibly. "I've got your shopping," he said, pointing to Paul's wire basket, lying in the corner, still full of oranges and bananas, canned peaches and figs. "Do you want to pay for it?"

46

"Yeah," said Paul, reaching weakly into his back pocket and giving him three pounds. "And a carrier bag."

"Carrier-bag – certainly," said the manager jovially. "We'll give you one of those on the house." And he was soon back with the change. Thinking "How soon can I get this young wally out of here? District Manager could come any moment. . . ."

"Is that an exit?" asked Paul, pointing to a door across the office, with a push-bar like the exit doors in a cinema.

"Exit, yes," said the manager. "Direct to the outside."

"I'll take it," said Paul, thankfully.

"What about the doctor?" asked Mrs Soames, in her trained nurse voice.

"He'll do," said the manager, thinking "Bugger the doctor – I'll cancel him – he won't be here for hours yet."

"Bye bye," said Paul, faintly; pushed the bar and found himself in a blessedly empty back-alley.

His main concern was to dodge people; but the gift of truth seemed to be getting worse. If he rested in one place more than a minute, people's feelings seemed to start oozing up out of the pavement through the soles of his shoes. Nasty, blurry feelings of hundreds of people who'd trodden on the place, all mixed up together; like the muddly kind of feverish nightmare when you can't get things sorted out. Certainly, the world was getting more and more *unreal*. He fell to hoping sincerely he'd wake up soon.

Then he tried walking on some grass. That was better; the grass, which was long and uncut, was happy, really happy. He sat down and luxuriated in the happiness of grass, as if he was sinking into a warm bath. Lay back . . . and then shot upright in terror. . . . And saw, fifty yards away, a metal railing, and a row of young trees, and a green gate, and a notice saying:

NO CYCLING IN THIS CEMETERY

Making his mind a blank, he ran on.

But at least he knew where he was running, now.

The old man had said, "I come sometimes and sit on this seat. If you need me."

He needed him.

And he was there; almost as if waiting for Paul, for he looked up with that wintry smile, and didn't seem at all surprised.

"Have you had enough of the absolute truth?"

"Yes."

"I have seldom heard someone so certain, so quickly. What about your wish to be a poet?"

"Bugger poetry," said Paul.

"You will settle for rugby football?"

Paul's heart leapt. "Yes!"

"You want me to take back the priceless gift of truth? Which hurts you? What about the priceless gift of life you gave me? That hurts me . . . will you take that back also?"

Paul trembled. "What do you mean?"

The old man laughed. "I am not asking you to murder me. No, we shall simply go back a little in time. I'm afraid you must lose the shopping you got for your mother, with so much effort. . . ."

Paul gaped; the carrier-bag full of groceries, which he'd laid on the seat, was gone. "But. . . ."

The old man laughed. "I am not a thief. Feel in your pocket."

Paul felt in his hip-pocket; his mum's three pounds were back. "What . . .?"

"We are moving back in time, you and I. Soon it will be the time before the lorry came down the hill. The time before you so brilliantly saved my life. Which I did not want saved. How did you come – to the place where you saved me?"

"I walked across the park, and turned right down the hill."

"Then go back to the park. Sit on a bench; bask in the sunshine; admire the sparrows. Until you hear . . . the lorry.

And when it is all over, you will come out of the park and turn left *up* the hill. And go to the supermarket the other way. You have had enough truth for one day, young man. Mankind cannot bear very much reality . . ."

"That's T. S. Eliot."

"A wise man, Eliot. Nearly as wise as me." The old man laughed, almost boyishly. As if he were looking forward to a treat.

"What *are* you?"

The old man shrugged. "All I will say is that it is not wise to meddle in the death of wizards. . . . Go now. I think you are a good young man – and I think you will have a happy life – as lives go."

Paul got up, reluctantly, as if he were about to commit a crime.

"Goodbye," he said, doubtfully.

"Good*bye*," said the old man, very firmly, but with a twinkle of affection.

Paul looked back once, at the park gate. The old man was sitting peacefully in the sun, head down.

He sat, and waited. The sun went briefly behind a cloud, and came out again. The trees swayed back and forth. There were no sparrows to observe. There was no way of telling whether time was running backwards or forwards. He was not wearing his watch; it was broken.

He jumped guiltily every time a car went past. But when the lorry came it was unmistakable. Big, driving fast, nearly out of control. Paul thought with pity of the driver; but the driver was *asking* for it, driving that fast.

The squeal of brakes; breaking glass. Then, after about three minutes, the wail of a police siren; then an ambulance siren. Then the ambulance going away, and more police-cars coming. . . .

Only then did Paul dare to move.

He couldn't bear not to look; the lorry was still there,

49

mounted up on the pavement, and there was a stain on the radiator grille that might have been blood or only dirt. The police were measuring the road, and there was broken glass from the lorry's headlight. He asked someone what had happened.

"Ran an old bloke down – killed instantly."

It was only when he got home from the supermarket, very late and Mam needing the bread for Dad's sandwiches, that he thought to look in his notebook.

The three poems were still there. An old man's gift. . . .

The three poems were accepted by Howard Sergeant, who said they showed real promise.

But he never wrote another one.

The Big Rock Candy Mountain

"... the soda water fountain,
where the lemonade springs and the bluebird sings
On the big rock candy mountain."
—American Folksong.

It should never have happened. They ought to have sailed straight on to Paris, France, where Hiram could've climbed the Eiffel Tower, strolled along the Bois de Boulogne with an independent air, cadged too much *vin ordinaire* out of Father at lunch, and watched in pleasant afternoon tipsiness the artists in berets and striped shirts painting execrable views of Notre Dame.

Instead, RMS *Aquitania* developed boiler trouble at Southampton, England. The Cunard Steamship Company offered all passengers another ship for Cherbourg, or they could stay safely aboard till the boilers were repaired. But Father remembered Aunt Mame. She had married a kilted hairy-legged Scotsman, who had carried her off to a castle in Kirkcudbright so soused in Scotch mist that she'd never been heard of again, except for a card every Christmas. Father was seized, while drinking a prelunch Gimlet, with an urgent desire to go visiting Aunt Mame. Why, Kirkcudbright was only three hundred miles ... a mere bagatelle. New York to Washington. Drive up one day, visit her the next, drive down

51

again the third. And still sail for Cherbourg on the *Aquitania*.

Once Father had made up his mind, he had the kind of terrifying persistence that could sink the *Titanic* all over again. Father had become a millionaire by making crazy decisions at a rate that left other tycoons gasping.

In half an hour they were standing on the quayside inside a small fortress of their purely essential luggage, while Father beavered his way into hiring a car. It was drizzling gently, with slight fog. Mom said it was always foggy and raining in England: part of the quaintness they ought to be enjoying. Hiram looked back longingly at the four funnels of the *Aquitania* and the rows of lighted portholes behind which they'd be serving lunch.

It turned out the British did hire cars – for funerals and weddings, and conveying people from the ships to the hotels, and from the hotels back to the ships. And always driven by uniformed chauffeurs; and within the boundaries of Southampton only.

Father called the American Embassy from a phone box, and exploded. Words like "John Jacob Astor" and "Stars and Stripes" came floating out . . . he was obviously talking to a Texan, because at one point he told him where he could stuff the Alamo. That, in Hiram's opinion, had definitely done it. Back to the *Aquitania* for lunch and deck-quoits.

So he was all the more amazed when eventually a huge car rolled out of the fog with blazing headlights; and an English voice so strangulated it could only belong to a duke enquired,

"Mr Hiram Schumaker?"

"The same," said Father. "Hiram Schumaker III and IV, Mrs Schumaker and Sonja. Put it there!" He held out a friendly hand to the fog and headlights. In response, a car door slammed and a figure was standing rigidly before him in peaked cap and highly polished knee-boots. Somehow Father's hand just withered back to his side.

The car was also impressive, with a bonnet like a Greek temple. It was so silent, Hiram thought the engine had stopped till he touched it and found the car gently quivering. In a trice, the chauffeur, whose name was Manners, had them inside, tucked under plaid travelling rugs. Father wanted to sit in the front to show Manners the way to Kirkcudbright. But somehow, Manners conveyed that was not *done* in England. You sat in the back and gave instructions through a brass speaking-tube.

"It's not *democratic*," exploded Father.

"I think Mr Manners finds democracy offensive, dear," said Mom. "He expects us to be aristocratic. Don't *lounge*, Hiram. Take that gum out of your mouth, Sonja!" They all sat stiff as ramrods, staring at the equally stiff back of Mr Manners through the glass screen.

It was the strangest car. Little tapestry curtains at all the windows, held back by gold cords; little silver flower vases screwed to the doors, with bouquets of fern and carnation. The seats were worn creaking leather; the rest was shining mahogany, like a sideboard. It smelt of champagne and wet dogs, tobacco and gunpowder. And the deplorable fact was that England would not keep *still*. It was all hills. If they were not going up, they were going down, which as anyone born in Chicago knows is a disgusting way to behave. Up and down they went, up and down, like that storm they'd met off the Grand Banks of Newfoundland.

"If you look out of the window, Hiram," said Mom, "you won't get sick."

Hiram, just in time, looked out and felt a little better. But England couldn't make up its mind what to be. First a village of black-and-white cottages, like a picture-postcard. Next minute, they were alone on a bleak moor, apart from a crowd of bored-looking sheep. Next, they were passing through a town as grim as Pittsburgh, with belching chimneys and white-faced people staring as blankly as the sheep had done. Then a golden cornfield, with a row of men moving in line with scythes, cutting the corn, as if McCormack had never invented the combine harvester.

53

All of which Mom found quaint, till Hiram could have screamed.

They had a late lunch at what appeared to be the Wizard of Oz's castle. Father asked Manners to join them, but he just quivered from head to foot, like a potential winner of the Kentucky Derby. The food was awful. Father said Manners wasn't being aristocratic; he just knew a better place to eat. Probably a place cabmen go.

Afterwards, Father, calling out the names on every sign-post they passed and consulting the road map which he'd borrowed from the first class library of the *Aquitania*, began to fret because they were falling behind schedule. It was already four o'clock and they were only halfway to Kirkcudbright. The car was fast; at one point on the open road they touched a hundred. But so little of the road *was* open. It didn't just go up and down, it also went left and right, frequently at right angles. As if it was afraid to cross a garden, or even a field, but must tiptoe round the outside, like a poor relation.

"The only long straight bits were built by the Romans," said Mom, "so the Ancient Britons couldn't hide round corners."

"Reckon the Ancient Britons won," said Father, bitterly.

Then there was the traffic; little flat carts pulled by trotting ponies; open carts selling milk straight into jugs from the churn; roofed carts selling massed ranks of oranges, apples and cauliflowers. Men with refrigerators on tricycles, selling ice creams under the legend *"Stop me and buy one!"* Through all this, the great car picked her way, as the *Aquitania* had picked her way through the tugboats of Southampton Water, gracefully but slowly.

And then the fog came back, making yellow haloes round the early gaslamps, which Mom found quaint. She even wound down her window a little (making sure that Mr Manners wasn't watching) and sniffed it ecstatically, announcing it smelt like a real London pea-souper.

"We are not going to London," said Father ominously, nibbling the ends of his Teddy Roosevelt moustache. "We are going to Kirk-cud-bright."

But it was not to be. The fog thickened, until each street-lamp was a long-awaited event. The voice-tube burped suddenly.

"I am endeavouring to reach the town of Northwich, sir. There's a reasonable hostelry called the Angel, where you can spend the night."

"The North *Witch*? Does she cast evil spells or something? Or does the Angel stop her?" Hiram realized Father was being jokey – a bad sign; he'd been hilarious the night before the Wall Street Crash.

"A *wich*, sir, is a salt-well, that provides an endless supply of brine, which the inhabitants boil off into salt to make an honest living." Mr Manners was at his British stiffest. But Dad thought he was being jokey, too.

"Yeah, yeah," he said. "We gotta song like that – The Big Rock Candy Mountain – lemonade springs and things like that! Good joke!"

"I have no knowledge, sir, of the folk customs of the United States of America. But we are approaching Northwich."

Hiram gaped. It seemed to him they were travelling up a narrow spit of land, between two endless lakes that faded on each side into the mist.

" 'On one side stood the ocean, and on one
Stood a great water, and the moon was full.' "

Mom often quoted the English poet, Alfred Lord Tennyson, when under stress.

"Where the hell's the moon," snapped Father, very Teddy Roosevelt. "I can't see the goddamn moon."

But Hiram wasn't listening. Something was looming out of the right hand lake, and it wasn't an arm clad in white samite, either. It seemed to be a tall factory chimney. And at its base,

55

pitifully drowned, the peaks of a row of factory buildings. Then the topmost branches of a dead tree. . . .

"Hey, Mom, floods . . ."

"Not floods, sir, subsidence. This is a subsidence area. The rocks below are pure salt for several thousand feet. When they pump out brine, great underground caverns form, then collapse, and the ground . . . sinks. The Northwich prophet, Nixon, predicted that one day Northwich will sink entirely under the sea. . . ."

"You mean, like, tonight?" gasped Mom.

"Unlikely, Madam. The best authorities think the process will take another several thousand years. . . ."

Northwich *leaned*. The fine church tower leaned gently west. Down the hill, the tall houses leaned a lot more, against great sloping beams of timber, like cripples on crutches. Pairs of houses leaned together, holding each other upright like drunken men. Great cracks ran down the walls, stuffed with rags, mud, plaster, anything to keep the draft out. Doors were set askew like a boxer's broken nose; windows slanted in opposite directions, like the eyebrows of an enraged dowager duchess. The narrow old road was a patchwork of filled-in holes, making the car leap like a bucking bronco.

"It's like the San Francisco earthquake, frozen halfway," said Father. He had been in a suburb of San Francisco as a boy, the day of the earthquake. He was very proud of the fact, and the family very tired of it. "How do the people stand it?"

But the people, far from merely standing it, were going about their business of selling fish and shaking hearthrugs quite cheerfully in their caps and shawls, as if nothing whatever was happening.

In the centre of it all, under a great flaring iron triple street-light, the car drew up.

"The Angel, sir! A fine old Georgian coaching inn."

It was a fine old inn, with Doric columns and many-paned

56

windows, and rosy light coming welcomingly through most. The only fault was, that like the *Titanic*, it was sinking by the bows. The left hand side was four feet below pavement level, and the right hand side at least ten. Roughly dug steps led down to the noble front door.

Mom took a deep breath and said, "Quaint!"

Father said, "Is it safe? It doesn't have any lifeboats!" Being jokey again.

"Safer than going on, sir!" said Mr Manners. And indeed the fog had thickened suddenly, billowing like clouds of steam, and reducing the triple street-lamp to three pale moons. They groped their way towards the hazy, rosy light that was now the only sign of the Angel. Inside, as good a lobby of polished mahogany, panelled from floor to ceiling, as anyone could wish. And a jovial landlord replete with beaming smile and red waistcoat. A pageboy to carry the bags, a roaring log fire. . . .

Of course it all sloped downhill to the right. Or did the ceiling slope down to the left? Certainly the fine grandfather clock leaned left, like the leaning tower of Pisa, though it was still going, with a loud, slow, reassuring tick.

Father braced his legs, as he had in the storm off the Grand Banks, and asked for rooms and dinner. He tried to book an equally good room for Mr Manners, but that worthy said he had friends in the town, and was already suited. From the set of his lips, his dislike of Democracy had not been weakened by circumstances.

After dinner, Hiram settled in his bedroom with his well-thumbed copy of *Huckleberry Finn* and a battered brass candlestick whose flame stuck out nearly at forty-five degrees. He sat on a stool by a cheerful flickering coal fire, and listened to the tick of the clock. The clock was sitting on the mantelpiece, its dial telling the wrong time, and a pendulum swinging behind a glass door. But the pageboy had told him it wasn't *meant* for telling the time. It was for listening to.

"You listen to the old clock, sir, listen to its ticking. 'Cos if her do stop, or the ticking changes, you get on your dressing gown, and get downstairs quick!"

"Oh, why?" Hiram had asked, as insouciantly as possible.

" 'Cos if her do stop, or change her tick, sir, it means this old inn's on the move again, down into the bowels of the earth."

"Pull the other leg," said Hiram sharply. "It's got bells on it!"

"Cross me 'eart, sir," said the pageboy. "That's why you'll find an old clock in every bedroom of this hotel, an' all telling a different time. Why, only the other night, sir, me and me brothers were tucked up four to a bed at 'ome, and our ol' clock stopped on the mantelpiece, an' afore we could move there was a rumble like someone tipping bricks outside. And when we all got outside,where our neighbours Mr and Mrs Yarwood had lived, there was just a hole in the ground. Mother, father, five kids, a cat an' a dog all vanished as if they'd never been. An' a canary. An' old Yarwood owed me Dad ten shillings – he'll have to dig deep to get it back now. Still, it saves the expense of buryin' 'em; they just got the vicar to stand in the 'ole and say a few words. . . . So listen to that old clock tick, sir. It's your best friend."

The trouble was, it was a *very* old clock. Every few minutes, when you were least expecting it, its old heart missed a beat. Hiram had gone belting downstairs five times already, only to find the grandfather in the lobby still ticking steadily, and a lot of men in cloth caps amiably drinking and playing shuffleboard.

But he had lost all desire to go to bed, let alone take his clothes off.

There was a tapping on the door, and Sonja came in.

"Can I sleep here? I don't like my room. I put my ball on the floor and it rolled uphill."

" 'Spect it'll do it here," said Hiram. They tried it, and the thing not only rolled uphill, but this way and that, as if it had a life of its own.

58

"Let's get out of here," said Hiram. "We can go buy candy, and get some fresh air."

"Fresh *what*?" asked Sonja. She stuck her head out of the window and smelled the fog, which reeked of soot and had a singeing salty smell.

But they wrapped up well in their coats and scarves and went, tiptoeing past Father and Mom, who were sitting with the cloth-capped men, buying them drinks in a democratic fashion, and being told such fearsome stories about subsidence and salt and floods that they noticed nothing. Hiram heard Mom say "How quaint" three times, with her hand to her throat, then they plunged out into the fog. They turned the corner, and ran into a scene like something out of Hell. A low rough wooden shed, stained white in patches. A great furnace roared in the middle of it, lighting great flat pans billowing steam with a fearsome red light, and huge full-bosomed women, stripped near naked, were drawing long rakes across the pans, drawing up great mounds of glistening wet white crystals. They ran on, before the women should notice.

The sweet shop seemed pretty normal. Mirrors running right up to the ceiling, advertising 'Five Boys' chocolate and 'Fry's Turkish Delight'. The shopkeeper knew what a dollar was; but he said they'd have to eat and drink a dollar's worth of sweets and what he called "hot sarsaparilla" on the spot, as he wouldn't give them any English change. Hiram thought the man a crook, but a pretty harmless and friendly and cheerful sort of crook, and he saw no reason why he shouldn't be as democratic as Father. So they sat down at a marble-topped table, and drank their hot red sticky glasses of sarsaparilla and tried all the kinds of sweets they could see on display, one after the other, till their dollar was used up. It seemed to be going a terribly long way, and he only hoped that Sonja wouldn't end up making herself sick.

The man asked them if they had cowboys where they lived,

and how much bother the Indians were, and if any of their family had ever been scalped. . . . Hiram thought he was kidding them. *Nobody* could be that ignorant. Then it was their turn to ask questions.

"Who was this Dixon the Prophet?"

"Not Dixon, Nixon," said the man. "Oh, you don't want to worry about Nixon – he's been dead donkey's years – before Good Queen Bess's time. Bess's granddad was called Henry, and he had to fight for the throne of England wi' a King Richard, and they fought hundreds o' miles away. Old Nixon was ploughing a field at the time, an' he suddenly began having a vision about King Henry and King Richard, and he prophesied King Henry would win an' King Richard be killed. An' a week later, a messenger came to the town to say that was exactly what had happened. And when King Henry heard, he sent for Nixon and made him his court jester. But Old Nixon had a prophecy about himself – that he'd starve to death. It worried him so much he took to sleeping in King Henry's pantry. An' when King Henry and all his court went away on holiday, they locked the pantry door, not knowing poor Nixon was asleep inside, an' he *did* starve to death in the end, pore soul. . . ."

"Don't you know any stories with happy endings?" asked Hiram snappishly. "Everybody in this town has miserable stories."

"Aye," said the shopkeeper cheerfully. "Us Northwichers are a bit down in the dumps usually. It's on account of Roaring Meg."

"Roaring who?" asked Sonja, her mouth agape.

"I expect she's the North Witch," said Hiram, bitterly.

"Lord love you, no. Roaring Meg's the great river o' brine that runs beneath this town, eating away the ground from under us. It was Roaring Meg that made those great lakes you'll have come across. . . . There's a story about that an' all. A pore milkman, wi' a horse an' cart was crossing that bit where them lakes are, when the earth collapsed . . . and neither him nor his horse nor cart were ever seen again. He's down there somewhere still. Bet his milk's gone sour by this time."

"I don't believe any of this," said Hiram, pointing to another bar of 'Five Boys' chocolate, with his mouth still full of the last.

"Oh, don't you?" said the man. "Well just come here an' listen." He opened a door, and switched on a light, and Hiram saw a flight of steps leading downwards. Hiram thought of men who enticed children away and murdered them. On the other hand, it seemed pointless to stuff the children full of chocolate and hot sarsaparilla first. So they went. Into the cellar. Where the man opened another door, on another downward flight of steps, and said, "Listen!"

And they listened, into the dank-smelling dark. And heard a rushing like a mighty underground river.

"That's Roaring Meg, doing her evil work," said the man.

But Sonja was staring round, big-eyed, with her thumb in her mouth. She took it out and said, "This is a funny room!"

And it was. It didn't look like a cellar at all, but like a grand sitting room, with a great marble fireplace and large windows . . . but the only things they could see out of the window were great balks of timber, holding back the earth. And there was rosy wallpaper hanging in damp strips off the wall.

"What *is* this?" asked Hiram.

"This, young sir, is the third storey of a gentleman's house. My shop is the top storey, the only one left above ground. But there are two more storeys below us, and a cellar. All sunk into the earth over the years. . . ."

Hiram gave him a hard look. But he didn't look shifty, or giggle. "I've heard too many strange things for one night," said Hiram.

"Then I'll tell you another," said the man. "Then you can go home to bed, and sweet dreams – if you can. There's a place called Winsford, a bit south of here, where there's a salt mine, dry as a bone. And in that mine, when the Czar of Russia came to see it, they held a Grand Banquet for him, with the ceiling lit by chandeliers, and all the tablecloths snowy white, and all the silver forks and glasses gleaming. For it's always warm and dry down there – dry as a bone – the salt takes the moisture out of the air, and it's fifty-six degrees Fahrenheit, night and day, winter and summer. . . ."

"Hiram – I feel sick," announced Sonja.

"Tek her home quick," said the man. "An' here's the rest of your chocolate bars to take with you.

Hiram thanked him, and somehow found his way back to the Angel. Sonja wasn't sick, and they got upstairs without Father and Mom even seeing them. Father was still being democratic, and even offering to sing Big Rock Candy Mountain. He'd obviously had more of a skinful than usual, and in this town, Hiram didn't blame him.

Hiram went to bed, but not to sleep; he kept all his clothes on, even his tweed overcoat and cap; and his big new-fashioned rubber electric torch by his hand on the eiderdown. Every time he closed his eyes, he became a slave to the ticking clock, which limped and stammered, playing with his nerves like a cat plays with a mouse.

"Damn Limey rubbish," he shouted, leaping off the bed and shaking it. But he hadn't even that consolation; it was an American clock, made by E. Ingraham of Bristol, Connecticut. He put it back on the mantelpiece, cravenly pleading with it to start ticking again. It obliged, and he closed his eyes. Must be near midnight.

A timid tapping. "Come in," he roared, much fiercer than he felt.

It was Sonja, also fully clad, eyes big as saucers, and clutching Hermione, the teddy bear she had long scorned, but kept on bringing on trips in a mood of pure forgetfulness.

"There's a man in my room," she said. "He keeps on tapping on the door and coming in."

"What *sort* of man? A waiter? A boot-boy?" Her greater terror made him feel bold, strong and scornful.

"No . . . a funny man, all raggy with long hair and a beard. He doesn't say nothing . . . just makes grunting noises."

Hiram's courage cooled rapidly. *Anything* could happen in this place . . . not like Chicago. With people like Al Capone, at least you knew what they'd do to you. A ragged grunty man might do *anything*.

"Go get Father."

"Father's room's round the bend in the corridor, and that's where the grunty man keeps hiding. . . ."

Hiram listened; through the whole sagging dark mass of the Angel there was now silence.

"Stay here with me. Get under the eiderdown." Under the eiderdown, with Hermione between them, it felt a *little* better.

"He won't *dare* come in here," said Hiram, quite failing to convince himself. "You've been dreaming!"

As if to contradict him, there came a soft tapping. Sonja hurled her arms around Hiram's neck and buried her face in his chest like they did in the movies; the effect was of being strangled. The door swung open, revealing only empty darkness in the dim and dying glow of the fire.

"You didn't fasten it properly," he shouted to Sonja, in a strangled sort of way. "It always swings open, with the inn sloping." He had almost worked up enough courage to go across and shut it, when the creature entered.

It paralyzed Hiram. It came silent, barefoot, softly as an animal. Like an animal, it leaped onto the dresser, crouched, and stared at them. It had a straggly beard and a shock of wild uncombed hair. It sort of *capered*, never still.

Then it stared at them again. Its rags were parti-coloured, green and brown, on arms and chest and legs . . . even in the firelight Hiram thought they were really red and yellow, under centuries of dirt.

They stared at it, and it stared back. Its eyes too were as big

63

as saucers, with the white showing all around, like a madman's. And yet it made no attempt to attack them. Rather, it seemed as timid as a rabbit. Hiram waved a fist fiercely, and it ran towards the door, whimpering. Then paused, and beckoned, urgently.

"It's . . . a sort of court jester," said Hiram.

"Maybe it's Dixon," suggested Sonja, who had allowed herself a furtive peep.

"Nixon," said Hiram; even near panic, he never missed a chance to put Sonja down. "But they said he'd been dead donkey's years!"

"He doesn't *look* dead!" said Sonja. "Maybe that shop-keeper was fooling us. Nixon! Nixon!" She called to the figure tentatively, as one might to a frightened cat. The figure responded by waving its arms wildly, and nodding its head so much they feared it might fall off. Then gestured them to follow him again.

"Hey, if he's Nixon the Prophet, maybe he's telling us the inn's going to fall down any minute!"

"Better warn Father. . . ." They followed the strange figure, who was anxious, as a cat is, to keep some distance between them. But at Father's door it pointed inside and shook its head with equal vigour.

"No, he just wants us!"

"Mom says not to go with strange men!"

"Call that a *man*? More like a monkey. *I* say, let's see where he goes. Maybe he wants to show us something."

They followed, down the dim stairs of the clock-ticking hall, Hiram clutching his torch fiercely, as if it was a club. As they turned on the landing, they saw Nixon vanish through a door at the back.

They went through that door; Hiram shone his torch round, with an authoritative flick. They were in the inn kitchen. Great sides of bacon hung from hooks like pale corpses; there were rows of cups, saucers, bowls, and things under white cloths for breakfast.

64

"He must be hungry *again*," said Sonja. "Perhaps he's inviting us to a midnight feast . . . after all that chocolate I ate . . . yuk!"

But of Nixon there was no sign, except another door darkly open beside the great fireplace. They investigated.

"He's down there," said Sonja. "I can hear him snuffling and shuffling."

"Ugh, smells damp." But they descended stone steps, gone slimy, by the light of the torch. And came to another kitchen, just like the one above. Only with damp sleeking the stone floor-flags, and the windows bricked up. But it *was* a kitchen: same big sooty fireplace, huge table, and iron pots and hooks for cooking. Only they were red with rust.

"It's the kitchen they had before the kitchen upstairs," whispered Sonja, "only it sank into the ground. . . ."

They stared uneasily at another open door by another fireplace, at steps leading down again into the dark, from which the snuffling and shuffling sounds came up. They went down.

"*Another* kitchen," said Sonja. "Three kitchens below each other." But here the big table was of stone, and all the floor and all the walls were white stuff, like a powdery fur. Hiram picked off a bit on his fingertip, licked it. "Salt, pure salt. Oozing out of the walls."

Across the floor, to another gaping dark door, ran Nixon's bare black footprints.

"How *many* kitchens?" breathed Sonja.

But the next was the last, and the open door led them out into a cobbled street; or rather a cobbled tunnel, because above the poor broken walls and windows was not the night sky, but a glistening arch of slimy, muddy rock.

"A whole street," breathed Hiram. "A whole *street* under the earth." His flicking torch beam picked out a wheelbarrow thrown on its side, with its load of white salt spilling out. There was an iron street-lamp, darkened for ever; and a child's iron hoop, nearly rusted through. And a low dark creeping shape that made Sonja scream because she thought it was a rat, but it was only a poor leather shoe, thick with mould.

Hiram threw the great beam of his torch along the short street; it caught a little prancing figure, who nodded and beckoned enthusiastically.

They ran towards him, but he flipped down over a ledge; as they ran up they noticed a sound of rushing water.

The end of the street was a little quayside, where two small boats had been tied up. But now one had been cast off and was whirling the summoning, beckoning figure of Nixon into a low tunnel.

"Hey, hold on," said Hiram. "So far, we can climb back, but . . ." He shone the torch down; the stream ran strongly and so clear they could see the rocky bottom; but it was bright blue, and little wisps of steam came off it.

"I guess this'll be Roaring Meg," said Hiram.

"Oh, c'mon," said Sonja, leaping down into the little rocking boat. "If Nixon can get back, so can we." She undid the chain that was holding it to the quay, and if Hiram hadn't jumped in, she'd have left him standing there.

There were no oars; the current simply swept them along. Hiram fretted; but Sonja sat there quite complacent, playing with the rusty chain. "I wonder if we'll find the milkman," she said thoughtfully.

Hiram swept his torch round and round in great arcs, trying to prove he was still master of the situation.

Now there were signs of human beings. Picks and shovels, coats hung on a wall, and caps hung above them.

"These must be the mines," whispered Sonja, "the abandoned mines."

"But why is everything crusted with ice?" whispered Hiram. "It's not even cold – it's quite warm, really." He couldn't even raise a shiver.

"Not ice, stupid – *salt*. Everything's encased in salt." And indeed, the great crystals, green and blue and yellow under the flashings of his torch, encased everything. The walls were walls of glass that reflected their little boat as they passed, so that they saw their own bodies and staring faces reflected, as if they too were encased inside the salt-ice, and lost forever.

Their boat stopped with a bump; they had run into the other boat, which was tied up to the bank with a chain again, and empty.

"Do we follow?" whispered Sonja.

"We certainly do follow," said Hiram. He flicked the torch up to where Roaring Meg ran on. She plunged through a narrow hole, and beyond there was the sound like a waterfall.

"No choice," said Hiram.

They scrambled ashore. The tunnel went high, so high the torch couldn't find the roof. There were cold drafts coming from many directions, so they knew they were in a huge cavern.

"Where now?"

"Follow the road," said Hiram.

For there was a little country road. It even had fences and gates on either side, and tall long-dead plants growing on the verges. And they came upon a quaint old high signpost, saying "Wincham, 2 miles."

But everything was encased in salt crystals.

"They use salt to preserve things," said Hiram, and shivered. "Salt will preserve anything."

"It's like a time-sandwich in the earth. . . . I wonder if we'll find the milkman."

"He was going to Wincham when . . ."

Then, far ahead, the beam of the torch fell on a cart standing in the road, with a milk churn in it. And something hunched-up beside the churn; and something else standing beyond the cart, that the torch couldn't reach. . . .

"Hiram, I'm scared."

"We gotta go on. There's no other way."

They went on tiptoe on the slippery salt-glazed road. They didn't mean to look up as they passed the cart but. . . .

There he was, just sitting there looking at them, his cap pulled right down over his ears, and his overcoat collar and muffler pulled up to his nose, and everything, even his nose, covered with salt crystals. And the horse, still standing, was covered with salt crystals, too. They just stared and stared in horror.

"Cold, for the time of year," said the milkman in a friendly way, like he wanted to be friends. And the crystals on his cap and muffler tinkled as he spoke.

"You're alive," said Hiram, stupidly.

"Aye, alive. Wondrously preserved by the salt. An' the horse, too." As if in agreement, the horse shook itself, as horses do. It sounded like a great glass chandelier, clinking musically in the draught.

"Are you looking for Nixon?" asked the milkman. "He passed not long since. He passes quite often in his travels. Brings me a bite to eat, and a bit o' hay for the horse. Sometimes newspapers, though they're always the wrong date. Sometimes too early, sometimes too late, so I can never tell what year it is. Still, it stops us getting bored. I tell the horse all the news – not that he understands much, but he sometimes shakes his head over the state of things."

"How can you *bear* it?" asked Sonja. "Down here?"

"Ha'n't got much choice, little missus," said the milkman. "I suppose it's the state to which God called me that terrible day in 1892, when the earth gave way. I'm luckier than some down here. I'm alive and can walk about a bit, though it's getting more difficult as these salt crystals get heavier. There're more people down here than ye might think, an' Nixon keeps us lively, wi' news o' what's happening up above. Then there're things like that feller all in black, wi' the gun. . . ."

"What fellow?"

"The one Nixon's following now. As I said, they came past not five minutes since, as far as I can tell the time in the dark. My pocket-watch stopped years ago."

68

"Thank you, sir," said Hiram politely. "Which way did they go?"

"Through Wincham, towards Winsford."

"Is there nothing we can do for you?" asked Sonja.

"You wouldn't have a bit o' tobacca? No, you're too young. Don't worry about me, little missus. You get used to it, after a bit. But if you see Nixon, tell him I could do wi' a glim o' candle."

They sped on; the tunnel began to slope upwards, the air to get drier. "Winsford," said Hiram. "Isn't that where the Czar of Russia . . . oh, my *God* – that man in black. He must be one of those Anarchists – the sort that throw bombs – he's going to try to assassinate the Czar. That's what Nixon's worried about. Hurry!"

They sped up the shallow slope. No more crystals now, just salt soft and white as snow underfoot, each separate grain winking in turn, in the light of the torch.

And then light was streaming down in front of them: the soft warm yellow light of candles. There was the tunnel mouth, and a great cave, with stalactites of salt dangling blue and green from the roof. But rich Turkey-red carpets had been strewn on the floor, and there were tables laid with sparkling white cloths, and candelabras full of candles, and silverware shining, and many men, some sitting, some standing, all in sombre black. All except a little group dressed in splendid blue and red with sashes and medals and golden stars on their chests.

"That's the Czar," said Sonja, "the one with the biggest beard."

And at that moment, from a side passage, stepped out a figure in a black cloak, with a broad-brimmed black hat, such as they had never dreamt of seeing outside a comic strip. And he raised a long pistol, aimed straight at the Czar's head. . . .

Nobody noticed, except Hiram and Sonja, and Nixon behind him, capering and frantic, but for some reason quite unable to *do* anything.

"Hiram – *deal* with him," shrieked Sonja. But Hiram was rooted to the spot, quite unable to move.

But something, maybe Sonja's high-pitched shriek, made a man look up from the table. And in an instant, three other men had stood up, quite blocking the Czar from view. And the next second, the Anarchist was struggling in the hands of three huge police constables in pointed helmets and tunics buttoned up tightly to their chins. Handcuffs clinked solidly, and he was led away.

Everyone sat back down at their tables, and, after a short pause, continued talking and eating. Even the Czar, though he did look a trifle pale and sweaty. Nobody noticed Hiram and Sonja; nobody seemed able even to *see* them. So they slipped out of the side tunnel, and walked around the Turkey-red carpet quite freely, slipping between the hurrying waiters. Sonja even tried to count the medals on the Czar's chest as he ate, but there were too many to count, the way he kept moving his arms about. Sonja wanted to take a plate of pork chops off the side table for the milkman, and some cabbage for the horse, but Hiram thought better not. And from another tunnel mouth, a grimacing, approving, winking, eyebrow-lifting, capering Nixon was beckoning it was time to go.

It took a long time, but they made it, climbing up through the endless kitchens of the Angel. And so to bed, each in their own room, for who could fear poor dear helpful Nixon now? They were quite sad to part from him; they waved and hoped one day to come and visit with him again. . . .

Hiram wakened late, even by his own watch, let alone that darned clock . . . well, at least the inn hadn't fallen into a hole during the night.

And then he remembered Nixon. God, what a *crazy* dream. All this crazy town! He drew back the curtains and stared out. The sky was that English grey like a workman's flannel shirt. You felt the clouds were resting on top of your head. The

70

buildings still leaned, like cripples on crutches.

It *had* been a dream, hadn't it? But it had left a heavy mark on his mind. And a heavy mark on his body too, like he'd been climbing and scrambling and burrowing and scraping all night. . . .

Better go and check up with Sonja; only he was reluctant, because she'd just laugh at him, and probably tell Father.

By the time he'd made up his mind, she wasn't in her room. She was downstairs already, breakfasting with Father.

They'd all come down late for breakfast, and sat late eating it. It wasn't just Sonja who looked worn out, thought Hiram. Mom and Father looked worn out, too. All that whisky and democracy. . . . The landlord kept on asking whether they'd like a little more bacon, or a little more toast or tea. (He didn't seem to have *heard* of coffee.) He didn't ask them whether they'd slept well either, which was very unusual for a landlord.

It was Manners who finally got them up from the table,, clean-shaven and immaculate in his newly pressed uniform and shining knee-boots, with a tartan travelling-rug over his arm, ready to tuck them in for the new day. "Your bags are packed and in the car, sir," he told Father, reprovingly. "We have a fair drive yet. And some interesting things to see. The Cumbrian Mountains, which are made entirely of green roofing-slate. . . ."

"*Roofing-slate?*" gasped Mom, giving him an old-fashioned look.

"Best roofing-slate in Britain, madam. And we pass the graphite mine at Keswick, where they mine the stuff inside all the lead pencils in the world."

"A *pencil mine*?" uttered Mom direly, the blood of her Pilgrim Fathers churning menacingly in her veins.

"And Gretna Green, on the Scottish border, where the blacksmith has the power to marry anybody, young or old, without a licence."

"Is he an *Episcopalian* blacksmith?"

"He will marry anybody, ma'am, Catholic, Buddhist or Seventh-Day Adventist."

"*Are* we half way to Kirkcudbright, Manners?" asked Father nervously.

"A little over half way, sir," said Manners, reassuringly.

"*Dear!*" said Mom to Father. "You have us half way through a *madhouse* . . . pencil mines, Buddhist blacksmiths, indeed! I never met your Aunt Mame . . . and what feelings of kinship I have for her are wearing pretty thin. When do we reach the Big Rock Candy Mountain, Manners, and the lemonade springs?"

"I have no idea of what you are speaking, madam!" said Manners, keeping his face deadly straight.

"*Dear!*" said Mom. "It may be cowardly, but I hear Cherbourg and Paris, France, calling. My cousin Elmer was there last spring, and he said *everything* was perfectly normal. Except the public conveniences, and at least they don't flush lead pencils or lemonade."

Father rose to the occasion like a man; he flicked back a lock of hair, twitched his moustache, looked his most Teddy Roosevelt and announced, "Next year, we do Great Britain, but *good* – a whole month. Drive us back to Southampton, Manners. I want to be back aboard the *Aquitania* in time for dinner."

"Sir," said Manners, without expression.

As they got into the car, Mom said "Hiram – your shoes are *soaking*."

Hiram hesitantly began to tell what had happened with Nixon the Prophet, but he soon faltered under his mother's eye and trailed off.

"Hiram," said Mom. "How can you bring yourself to tell such whoppers. You *dreamed* it."

"Didn't. That's why my shoes are wet."

"Then why aren't Sonja's, since she's supposed to have been with you?" They all looked. Sonja's shoes were bone dry.

72

"Such *stuff*," said Mom, and settled down inside her tartan rug to watch out for the next horror that Great Britain might sling at her. "Too much chocolate you had, young man – *and* too much hot sarsaparilla. But that inn was enough to give anyone nightmares. I forgive you. Drive on, Manners."

But every now and then, Hiram kept glancing at his shoes. An odd thing was happening. As they dried, they were turning white. Great white patches grew across them. Tiny crystals glistened. He put his finger down, then licked it.

Salt.

He looked up, and caught his traitorous sister's eye. She grinned and opened her bag. Inside was one shoe, and that was turning white as well. He gaped.

"I changed my shoes," she mouthed silently, across Mom's uncomprehending face.

"Why?" he mouthed back.

"Why upset them?" She pulled a face at Father and Mom. Father and Mom never saw; they had found something else quaint.

"So you were there all the time?"

She nodded with a conspiratorial grin, as the great car began to climb Salisbury Plain.

"If this is a *plain*," Father asked Manners, "why are we climbing?"

"I have no idea, sir," said Manners, keeping his neck very still. "We should have a sight of Stonehenge in a moment."

"Next year," said Father, "I'll sort out you British. We'll take a whole month, I *swear* it!"

Mom shuddered delicately, as the car swept on towards Southampton, the *Aquitania*, dinner and sanity.

Author's Note

I made up Hiram and his family, Manners, and Hiram's dream. All the rest, about England and Northwich, is

73

Rachel and the Angel

Rachel sat on her bike in the vicarage gate, twisting the handlebars and watching the front wheel screw up dust. The tyre was flattish, but she couldn't be bothered to pump it up. It was half past nine in the morning and already too hot. Still cool in the shadow of the vicarage oaks, but beyond, the village street burned, little stalks of yellow straw chasing their tails in the heat eddies. A car passed, going into the village too fast, blatting Rachel sideways with a gust of burning air. She regained her balance just in time and went on sitting.

Which way should she go? Back to the empty vicarage, the cold tap dripping on greasy plates in Mum's disorganised kitchen? She could wash up, but Mum would take it as criticism. Besides, the kitchen frightened her a bit when Mum wasn't there. Mum took her zany sense of humour with her, and left only the chaos.

No point going back. Or turning left, either. Beyond the vicarage trees the cornfields started, a heartless sea of gold, rising and falling, without hedges or shade, without cottages or gardens, people or animals, or even birds. The road crept through it, fenceless, like an unwanted dog, all four miles to Stensfield. On that road she'd see nothing but the distant lines of combine harvesters, eating up the wheat in square blocks like cornflake packets, spewing out their endless vomit of grain. You couldn't even see the men inside. On bad days she had the feeling the machines were doing it by themselves.

No point turning right, either. Beyond the rim of council houses, the cornfields bit into the village again. The village was drowning in a sea of gold, like a pretty head without a body any more. It didn't used to be like this. When she was little, Daddy had taken her for walks. There'd been woods, birds and hedgehogs.

All gone; swept away by the corn.

Only in front was there any life; the village street leading up to the church. If she rode slowly, there might be time for Dr Diggory to pass, toot, pull up and ask how she was, this fine morning? Then she'd lean her arm on the hot roof of his car, and they'd discuss something he'd just read in the *Telegraph*. Dr Diggory was old, at least fifty, with a stiff, lined face that had watched too much pain. But talking to him made her feel grown up for half the day afterwards.

But most mornings, he didn't pass. Of course she could turn at the church and ride slowly back, giving him a second chance. But if she did that too often, the village women gossiping at their gates would notice and start gossiping about *her*.

Or she could go to the antique shop. Mrs Venn let her help with dusting and talked to her about the deeper mysteries of porcelain. Sometimes, if Mrs Venn had been to a sale, there'd be new treasures to unpack and admire. Mrs Venn was a widow and nearly as old as Dr Diggory. No chicken, Mum said. Yet she was as pretty and cheerful as a married woman half her age, with her short blonde hair and marvellous blue eyes. She had no children; she had nobody. Yet she had this happiness she shared with Rachel, as easily as she might share a seat on a bus.

But Rachel had spent all yesterday at the antique shop . . . don't spoil a good thing, a little warning voice said.

Go and see Ziggy? Who lived below the church with his huge garden and tiny cottage, one room up, one down? Good job Ziggy was so tiny or he'd never fit in. Ziggy and Molly were both small enough, because Molly was a fat black and white cat. Though when Rachel had first heard him talk about her, she was sure Molly was his wife. Ziggy talked to Molly constantly, quarrelled with her bitterly at times. Rachel remembered coming up to the garden-gate, hearing Ziggy's high-pitched shouts of "Mowderer, mowderer!" And there was poor Molly, cowering beneath the giant cabbages with a dead blackbird tied round her neck as if she was the Ancient Mariner. . . . Or Molly huge with kitten, while Ziggy raged at her about the Catholic virtue of chastity. "She is no better than a street-stroller, Miss Rachel!"

But between them, they always found homes for the kittens.

Ziggy was Polish, a flotsam of war, who'd appeared in the village in 1946, miles from any other Pole. Sometimes he talked of going home, to his sister who was a professor in Poland. Then he'd shake his head and say, "Poland is Poland no more, Miss Rachel. If I went back there, I wouldn't know it." So, instead, each summer, his garden would blaze with the colours of the Polish flag.

"So this is Poland now, Miss Rachel!"

Or there'd be other flowerbeds, in the colours of the Pope or the Virgin. "See, I am faithful to the Church, Miss Rachel. Even if they are not faithful to me because I drink too much!"

He made a living as a jobbing gardener, and every year won the prize for the biggest marrow. But she couldn't take Ziggy this morning. It was nearly time for the village show and he would talk of nothing but marrows. "Jack Sprigg's marrows, they are not well, I hear. Always they start well, but they fail. Perhaps they see Ziggy's marrows and lose heart!"

No, no marrows this morning.

Suddenly she realised there was nowhere in the world she wanted to go. It made her feel quite desperate. The blinding August sunlight closed in like a black cloud. Daddy and Mummy, gone to lunch with the Bishop, wouldn't be home till four. Time stretched ahead like a black sunlit tunnel.

In that instant, there was a shattering double bang overhead. Before she could flinch, she saw the two planes vanishing across the rooftops at the end of the village, curving up across the swelling corn. Phantoms, from the US airbase, eating up the blue sky like the combines ate up the fields, leaving behind their foul transparent tails of black smoke and the disgusting smell of a badly trimmed paraffin heater. Evil, with all the black pointed darts under their wings; devils from Armageddon. Breaking the rules, flying too low as usual. She had a sudden impulse of black hate, to ring up the base and complain, get them into trouble. But there would just be the usual calm and maddeningly reasonable American voice at the far end, assuring her the matter would be looked into, ma'am. Making her feel a silly little fuss-pot.

She knew she must do something quick, or she'd get into one of her black moods. Once she was in a black, she'd be a week getting out of it, and they *hurt*.

The church; she'd go to the church, always her final refuge. Half-way down the village street, on the corner by the post office, she passed a group of kids her own age, from the local comprehensive. The girls looked at her, then flounced their pathetic blue and green hair and turned their backs, as if to say 'stuck-up bitch'. One boy, the tall dishy one who delivered the milk in the holidays, gave her a smile. When she was past, another boy, she was *sure* it was another boy, gave her a rather rude wolf-whistle. But they'd never do anything about it. Farmhand's son and vicar's daughter . . . in this part of Lincolnshire? She might as well have been a green-eared Martian.

Nonetheless, her face burned all the way to the church. The sound of the petrol-driven motor-mower told her old Moley, the sexton, was cutting the grass between the gravestones. Thank God he was out of sight, around the back of the chancel.

*   *   *

78

She swung the oak door shut behind her. The heavy clink of the iron latch was a comfort. She breathed in the air of her private kingdom; mildew and candles, incense and dusty hassocks. Dim and cool; but not as cool as she'd hoped. Daddy said the church stayed cool for a week in a heat wave; then the thick stone walls gave back their heat like storage heaters.

The tower-base was friendly. The striped sallys of the bell-ropes threw their looped-up shadows across the bell-ringers' notices; a stone tablet, recording the ringing of Triple Bob Major to celebrate the old Queen's Jubilee; yellowing cartoons of bell-ringing monks, fastened to the panelling with rusty drawing pins.

Once when she was eight, greatly daring, she'd unlooped the sally of the smallest bell, the service bell, and rung it three times before it snatched itself from her hand. She'd caught it and rung it nine times more; before a crowd of villagers rushed in, frantic to know which child of nine had died?

But today the sallys held no excitement; they looked dirty, like the tails of dead lambs. She could not shake off her blackness.

She walked on; stood beneath the great royal coat of arms that hung on the gallery. The village had paid a lot of money to have it carved in 1661, to prove their loyalty to the new-returned king; even though five village lads had died for Cromwell. She moved her head this way and that, letting the light from the windows bloom blue in strange patterns across the dark polished oak.

But it didn't help.

She went and stroked the coolness of her alabaster knight, where he lay with crossed legs and great mailed arm ever reaching across to draw his sword. Centuries ago, the village men had carved their initials in his soft stone; knocked off his nose to grind up as a cure for sheep-colic.

But this morning he had nothing to say to her.

79

She didn't feel like playing her usual games; didn't feel like sitting in the choir stalls and singing the 'Nunc Dimittis', listening to her small voice echoing round the angel roof, as if all the great carved angels were singing too. She didn't feel like finding and reading out loud the lesson for the day at the great brass eagle of a lectern. Didn't feel like playing the organ, or even mounting the shockingly high pulpit and preaching one of daddy's favourite sermons, complete with every wickedly mimicked 'um' and 'ah'.

Silly, empty, childish games. The church's deep sloping windowsills were thick with the bodies of small black flies, as usual. Why were they born in here, only to die trying to hammer their way out to the light of day? She brushed them off from habit; under her hand they mixed with the dust that always came off the limestone sills. By the time they hit the floor, they were no more than grey dust themselves.

As a last hope, she climbed into the south gallery, to look at the roof-angels. Carved in oak, bigger than a man, their intricate wings stretched out to touch each other across the rafters. Remote calm faces and flowing hair. But all exactly alike. How could the old carver have borne to carve each face exactly the same, year after year? And though their shapes were beautiful, the wood was a dull grey-brown, and thick dust lay in every crevice of their robes. And the rest of the gallery was stuffed with old burst kneelers, and tawdry hoopla-stuff from the village fête, and bundled-up Union Jacks from the coronation of 1953.

Nobody came up here but her. Not enough congregation to fill half the floor of the nave.

Dullness. Five hundred years of dullness. She could've screamed. If only something wonderful or terrible would happen, just once. Instead of dusty wooden angels, a *real* angel, like in the Bible. . . .

In that instant, though she'd heard no one come in, she knew she was no longer alone in the church. Her arms and legs began to shake in the most peculiar way. Trying to control them, she tiptoed down to the front of the gallery. Even so, the dry boards creaked and cracked under her feet.

She could see all the opposite gallery and aisle, and the floor of the nave. Nothing stirred, not even a fly. The sun was streaming in through the south aisle windows beneath her feet, making pools of sunlight on the slabbed floor. If anything moved beneath her, she'd see the shadow.

Nothing moved . . . the bell-sallys hung quite motionless in the tower-base, telling her no one had opened the church door.

That only left the chancel and the altar.

There was something to the left of the altar that hadn't been there on Sunday. That had never been there before. Beyond the altar-rail that Mrs Munslow polished weekly, as if her life depended on it. Beyond Lady Wilbrook's grand but dying flower arrangement. Beyond the massive gold candlestick with its spiring white candle was something new and tall and dark. . . .

Of course there'd be a perfectly sensible explanation. Always was. Not at all sure she wanted a sensible explanation, with a dark delicious fear squeezing her belly, she clumped down the gallery stairs like an elephant in hobnailed boots, as Mummy would have said. At the bottom, the only thing in the whole church she hated caught her eye. The Ten Commandments, lettered on the wall in a huge black Gothic script that crawled like spiders.

THOU SHALT NOT COMMIT ADULTERY

Mummy said those who committed adultery were called adults. Stifling a wild giggle, and with her guts still deliciously shrinking, she walked echoing up the aisle towards the altar.

As she got nearer, her steps slowed. She craned her neck, trying to peer past the huge flower arrangement, expecting every minute that the thing would become quite ordinary. It didn't. Even when she was past the altar-rail, it refused to turn into anything sensible. Now she was only three feet away and it was the oddest thing she had ever seen.

Taller than Daddy; almost seven feet high. Curvy, sharp-edged and a shining brown, with a purply glint where the light from the windows caught it. Must be metal; bronze. It was precisely cut and detailed, like a new coin, and she thought it *extremely* ugly. It seemed to have . . . wings. Three sets of wings, not so much feathered . . . more like the scales on a snake. Each pair of wings was folded; the top pair across where a face would be, the second across the body and the third across the feet.

She wasn't a vicarage child for nothing. She knew the Bible text.

"And with twain they covered their feet and with twain they covered their face and with twain they did fly."

It was supposed to be a statue of an angel; modern art! Soft old Daddy had let some crazy modern artist dump the monstrosity on him, because nobody else would have it. God knew what the church council would say . . . they'd nearly gone mad when he introduced the second set of altar-candles. And when he used incense, once a year at Christmas, they all coughed like they were dying of pneumonia and the Russians had launched a poison-gas attack. Oh, *Daddy!*

She walked round it, pouting in disgust. The stupid artist had plastered the back with what looked like eyes, in the most revolting sort of way. That was in the Bible, too, of course.

"Covered with eyes, without and within." The eyes weren't bronze, but huge and shiny and dark like camera lenses. And clustered as thick and ugly as the spots on Derek Wharmby's cheeks . . . yuk!

But she couldn't resist reaching out to touch.

Two inches away, heat hitting her fingertips made her pull back. It wasn't icy-cold like bronze, but red-hot, like the church stove in winter.

Don't be *silly!* She reached out and touched it.

And blistered her finger. She leapt back a yard and sucked her fingertip and watched the thing. The waves of heat

82

coming off it made her break out into a sweat. Where a couple of leaves of Lady Wilbrook's flower arrangement touched it, they had crumpled and died. No wonder the church felt so warm!

Some new sort of central heating system, going full blast in the middle of a heat wave. How crazy could you get? It must have cost a bomb to make. . . .

Suddenly it all got too much. It was Daddy's worry, not hers. She began to walk away down the church. She hadn't got as far as the chancel steps when there came a strange creaking rustling behind. She whirled in a panic.

The wings were slowly opening. They might touch the altar-hangings and set them on fire! Exasperated, close to tears, she ran back. And saw the most horrible thing. As the wings opened, the body she had thought was shining bronze began to wrinkle like skin, and she knew with horrid certainty it was alive.

The opening wings disclosed more pimply shining eyes, all over the face and body. And they began to glow dimly. And then they glowed brighter and brighter, until they were like the little red holes in a workman's brazier. As if the whole creature was full of fire. Black stalks extending from the head, like snail's eyes.

Oh, it must be a bomb, a missile from the air-base. She must fetch old Moley the sexton, the police, the fire-brigade. . . .

But as she ran down the church, it seemed to stretch to an infinite length, as if the great stone arches were made of elastic and she might run for ever and ever. And then the aisle seemed to twist to the left and downwards, and she tripped over her own feet and fell.

If she had nursed the hope that it was all a bad dream, the pain in her knees, the trickle of blood down her white shin told her it was not. She twisted round, where she lay, to look back towards the altar. The dark figure seemed to fill the chancel arch. The altar seemed to have shrunk to the size of a silk-covered stool. The very fabric of the church seemed to be bending, as if trying to get away from the figure.

She knew she could not.

"I AM ZAPHAEL." The name was inside her skull like a clap of thunder, though she was oddly certain it hadn't got there through her ears. She was on her knees before it, because her legs simply refused to stand up. She felt she was going to be sick. She felt outraged at what this thing was doing to her and to Daddy's church. A small furtive part of her mind still played with the idea of getting a big hammer and smashing it. But already it was filling her mind again.

"I BEHELD SATAN AS LIGHTNING FALL FROM HEA-VEN." It held no trace of joy or regret, no emotion at all, like a speaking clock. Less emotion than a speaking clock, for that at least *tried* to sound friendly. This just filled her mind until she feared it would burst apart with the strain.

"THERE WAS WAR IN HEAVEN. MIKEL AND HIS ANGELS FOUGHT AGAINST THE DRAGON AND THE DRAGON FOUGHT AND HIS ANGELS AND PREVAILED NOT NEITHER WAS THEIR PLACE FOUND ANY MORE IN HEAVEN AND THE GREAT DRAGON WAS CAST OUT INTO EARTH AND HIS ANGELS WITH HIM."

From her place on the floor, she looked at the scaly bronze skin, as it rose and fell, wrinkled and twitched, and she shuddered. She had forgotten that the devils had been angels once. Once, before they fought, they must all have looked very much alike . . . been very much alike. Not human; not human at all. All those silly artists carving them and painting them looking like women with beautiful faces and long golden hair and graceful white hands playing harps and trumpets . . . if only they'd bothered to look in the Bible for the real descriptions . . . the Burning Bush, that Moses feared to look upon, that was not consumed . . . *that* had been an angel. . . .

She felt the heat of the thing on her face, even from this

84

distance. It was glowing like a black cage of fire, like a volcano about to erupt, and throw down the whole village.

She didn't even know which side this one had been on, Mikel's or Satan's. There was no way of telling. It must have been a terrible fight between Mikel and Satan . . . she had seen two tomcats fighting on the roof of the garage, the tangled twisted screaming rolling over and over, the blood the tufts of ginger fur streaming from them like autumn leaves on the wind . . . how much more awful Mikel and Satan . . . their wounds. . . .

"THE DRAGON FOUGHT . . . THE DRAGON FOUGHT . . . THE DRAGON FOUGHT. . . ." Now the creature sounded like a speaking clock that was breaking down, going wrong. Its head was lopsided. Had *it* been wounded, dreadfully wounded?

"BEHELD SATAN . . . BEHELD SATAN FALL . . . SATAN FALL."

There was something dreadfully wrong with the creature. It was not just terribly powerful, but terribly going wrong. Like an elephant running amok . . . it might . . .

"THIS CITY IS UNDER JUDGEMENT. I WILL DESTROY THIS CITY. I WILL DESTROY THIS CITY UTTERLY."

"But *why*?" Her voice was a wail. "What have we done?" It never occurred to her to question the thing's power.

"THIS CITY IS AN ABOMINATION OF WICKEDNESS."

"You can't destroy us . . . it wouldn't be allowed."

"HAVE YOU FORGOTTEN SODOM?"

"You can't . . . we know too much now . . . the whole world would notice . . . these things don't happen any-more. . . ."

There was a long hot silence. And then, in the hot silence, there was a familiar double bang overhead. Tiny trickles of dust fell from the ceiling, through the beams of coloured sunlight from the stained glass windows. The Phantoms from the air-base had come back. Still flying suicidally low. God knew what destruction they held in those evil dart-shapes under their wings. . . .

And if the pilots made one split-second mistake . . . the village . . . if this creature even made the pilots blink . . . of course there would be a court of inquiry afterwards . . . regrets expressed . . . new regulations made . . . compensation paid. But Mummy and Daddy, Dr Diggory, Mrs Venn, Ziggy, and the boy who delivered the milk in the holidays would be tiny shapes under tarpaulins, shrunk by the heat of the inferno, if they still existed at all. No bigger than charred dolls. . . .

She did the bravest thing she'd ever done, then. She rose to her feet, patted her hair back in place and said to the dark shape, "I don't believe in you. I have made you up. You are only in my mind. I've been . . . upset lately . . . alone too much. I read the Bible too much. I hear about God's wrath destroying the world nearly every day. I am frightened of the American bombers because they fly too low. I shall go and fetch people now. If you are still here when I come back, they will photograph you and put you in the papers and do experiments on you. You won't like that. And if you aren't here when I come back, I will know you never really existed."

She knew she was being unfair; she wanted to be unfair to it.

It said nothing.

She turned and walked away.

She was afraid the church would start to stretch and twist again, but it didn't. The slabbed aisle stayed firm beneath her feet. Oddly enough the outside door was slightly open, letting in a bar of sunlight across the rough coconut matting of the tower-base. She thought she'd shut it when she came in, but the latch mustn't have fallen properly and the wind had blown it open again. For some reason she slid through the gap without touching the door. . . .

It was the silence that struck her first. Not a country silence touched with a rustling of leaves, a passing car or the distant lowing of a cow.

86

Total utter silence; the silence of a tomb.

And then the utter stillness struck her. The leaves of the silver birch by the lychgate had been blown back by the wind, showing their pale undersides. But the wind had gone, and still they stayed blown back, frozen. Frozen like the chimney-smoke of Miss Mulbridge's cottage, where she kept a fire burning winter and summer to heat the kettle for a cup of tea. Frozen like the clouds which looked painted on the blue sky.

Nothing in the whole world moved; yet still she ran for the safety of old Moley, the sexton. She noticed as she ran that the gravel of the path didn't scrunch under her feet. It felt fixed, immovable, as it did in a hard frost. The bumps in it hurt her feet through her sandals, like frozen ruts. She turned the corner of the chancel, and saw old Moley. He was just curving the motor-mower round the edge of the Granville tomb, head on one side in neat calculation, tongue half-out with concentration, the beads of sweat standing out on his brow under the faded Panama hat. He had one foot off the ground, taking a step; the cut blades of grass flew from the front of his mower. But all, foot and sweat and blades of grass in mid-air, were frozen into stillness. She tiptoed closer; his chest wasn't moving; he wasn't breathing. Unless he breathed soon, he would die . . . she touched him. He didn't even rock on his feet; he was as immovable as a marble statue. She even tried to push one of the blades of grass that were suspended in mid-air. It not only stayed in position, unmoving; it cut her finger like a razor-blade.

Zaphael had frozen the whole world.

But that meant everything was dead already.

Or else . . . Zaphael had taken *her* out of time itself. She was caught with Zaphael alone, forever in one moment of time. She could run as far as she liked through this frozen world; she would find no help, no food, no water.

The only thing to do was to go back into church and face him.

*   *   *

87

Zaphael was standing where she had left him. His wings were still open, unfolded, but the light in his eyes was very dim. He might have been asleep.

But her mind was racing; the mind of a church-child who had heard the Bible read, Old and New Testament, since she could first remember anything. And suddenly she saw a trick that might work. She shouted, "Do *you* remember Sodom?"

The creature heard her; slowly its eyes lit up again, as she stood shouting at it, trembling with fright and eagerness.

She knew it remembered the destruction of Sodom.

"Do you remember Father Abraham? Do you remember his bargain with God?"

It remembered; its eyes glowed brighter and brighter until they were almost white with heat, until she feared she would melt with sweat, and the whole church burst into flame.

"Do you remember God's promise? *Do* you? That if Father Abraham could find ten good and just men in Sodom, God would not destroy it?"

Zaphael was silent; but she knew he remembered.

"There are good people *here* . . ." Sensing victory within her grasp, she felt so tense she was about to burst.

Zaphael was silent; she might almost have thought that Zaphael was waiting for something. Waiting for her . . . to. . . .

Name the first name. She named it, feeling as if she was playing the first card in her hand at the parish Christmas Whist Drive.

"Ziggy," she said, not wanting to play her trump-card too soon.

Suddenly she was in a different place. A small familiar room, only made unfamiliar by the light of an oil lamp and a fire in the grate. Ziggy's kitchen, and the curtains drawn, and Molly sprawled contentedly in the wooden rocker, her head hanging out on one side and her feet and tail hanging out the other. Ziggy sat in the other wooden rocker, on the other side of the fire, battering at some liquid in a rusty old saucepan, with a big wooden spoon.

Both Ziggy and Molly looked at her in such a natural way that she said, "Hallo Ziggy! Hallo, Molly!"

Ziggy looked straight through her, and went back to battering the contents of the pan, warming it occasionally over the red coals of the small summer fire. Only Molly really saw her, the big green eyes following every move she made, the black-and-white ears flying in all directions, semaphoring alarm.

"I'm a ghost," thought Rachel. "Zaphael has made me into a ghost. Only cats can see ghosts. . . ." It was all so absurd, she felt like giggling.

But now Ziggy was on his feet, spoon put down on one side of the brick fireplace.

"Now we shall see! Now we shall show them!" he said, triumphantly. Rachel started with alarm, then realised he was only talking to Molly as usual. She watched while Ziggy fetched a large black polythene bucket full of water, and squeezed the contents of the pan into it, through a yellow plastic colander. "Ah, good, good" he murmured to himself, stirring vigorously. "And a good night of raining to do it."

Only then did Rachel notice the whispering drumming of rain on the thatched roof of the cottage. But by that time, Ziggy was pulling on black wellies, a black rubber mackintosh like the vets wore, and even a black sou'wester. He looked comical, like a miniature black version of a lifeboat cox'n off a box of matches. He looked even funnier when he lifted from the corner of the kitchen an old wartime stirrup pump, the kind they used to put out incendiary bomb fires. . . .

Then he went out into the dark and the rain, closing the door and locking it carefully. Rachel, who had by this time got back some of her sense of humour, decided to see if she really was a ghost who could pass through doors . . .

She passed through quite easily, and followed Ziggy into

the night. She betted to herself that Molly's ears must be semaphoring like mad. . . .

Outside, Ziggy stumped along through the rain, bucket in one hand, and pump in the other. Rachel realised it was very late; all the lights in the cottage windows were out; the village was fast asleep. Ziggy stumped till he came to a high, well-trimmed hawthorn hedge. Rachel recognised the sagging white gate.

Jack Sprigg's house. For the first time, the whole thing stopped being comical. Rachel felt a slight twinge of unease, as if Zaphael had reached out a cruel black iron hand, and gripped at her stomach.

Ziggy bent to his bucket and pump. He put the end of the pump into the bucket of black liquid, and began to pump the handle. A thin jet of black water shot upwards, fighting against the heavy falling rain. It went high over Jack Sprigg's hedge and curved down into Jack Sprigg's garden. Rachel heard it pattering down on big flat leaves, heavier than the rain, but disguised by the rain . . . as Ziggy was disguised in the darkness by his black raincoat and sou'wester. What was happening was invisible, inaudible, to Jack Sprigg in his cottage, whether he was in bed snoring, or awake, alert for intruders.

There was a thrumming, drumming, as if the black water was falling on some big hollow drum-like object. . . .

Like a prize marrow.

Somehow Rachel knew that this year again, Jack Sprigg's marrows were going to lose heart.

In her mind, Rachel started to argue with Zaphael. C'mon, what's a few marrows? You can't destroy a village for a few marrows. . . .

But she had to go on following Ziggy round. From garden to garden; from that of the greatest marrow-growers to the very weakest poorest marrow-growers who had no *chance* of winning. And everywhere, like a demon worm that flies in the night, the black rain fell within the clean rain, on the marrows. Until not one was left untouched. Though the clean rain would wash off every trace of black from the leaves, the black would be in the soil. And Ziggy worked so thoroughly, with such crouched intentness, like a murderer over his victim, like a weasel at the throat of a rabbit . . . his very intentness grew hateful.

And then she was back in the sunlit church. Zaphael, at the far end, was still, unmoving. He might have been asleep. But she was standing opposite where the Ten Commandments were written in black spidery letters on the wall.

THOU SHALT NOT COVET THY . . .

Thou shalt not covet thy neighbour's marrow, thought Rachel, sadly.

"All right," she said, taking a deep breath. "Mrs Venn." She would save Dr Diggory till next. Dr Diggory was an even stronger card. Dr Diggory got up in the middle of the night to old ladies who were no more than lonely and frightened. Dr Diggory saved babies' lives. People said Dr Diggory was a saint.

Suddenly, she was in Mrs Venn's shop. This time it only gave her a slight jump, though again the two people in the shop looked first at her, then through her. She was getting used to it.

This isn't today, thought Rachel, because it's raining and grey outside, a miserable afternoon. Mrs Venn had the lights on. And Rachel knew it was at least last week, because the grandfather clock was still there that Mrs Venn had sold last Friday.

The other woman in the shop was called McNab. She was at least eighty and the nastiest, cattiest old woman in the village. Everybody loathed her. Even Mum said that some old people made their own loneliness.

Both women were staring at a black, gold and orange plate that had for untold years hung on Mrs McNab's wall, just inside her front door. Which was usually open to the village

91

street, so Mrs McNab didn't miss anybody who went past, so she could grab them to do her an errand. Mrs McNab had been known to have five neighbours doing her shopping for her at once. Each shopping for one item, they kept bumping into each other. Anyway, Mrs Venn and Mrs McNab were staring at the gold, orange and black plate, like it was a beloved pet about to expire.

"It's a real antique," said Mrs McNab. "It was bought for me grandmother by me grandfather the week after they got married. My granny used to give me my cakes off it, when I wasn't five years old."

"When was your granny married?" asked Mrs Venn, with a sort of weary compassion.

"It were . . ." Mrs McNab did mumbling calculations, her lips trembling, the little black whiskers on them shaking. "It were eighteen eighty-seven . . . no, I tell a lie . . . eighteen eighty-eight . . ."

"That's not very old for an antique," said Mrs Venn gently. "They're supposed to be a hundred years old. And it's part of a set . . . you haven't got the rest?"

"When me granny died, all her daughters got a bit of the set . . . it were split up between 'em . . . and me mam broke t'cup and saucer when me dad got . . . ill."

Mrs Venn pulled a wry face, behind the old lady's back. Everyone knew the old man had got his illness out of a bottle. "And I'm afraid it's rather chipped," she said gently.

"Just round the edge," said Mrs McNab defensively. "And I got our Billy to touch it up wi' a lick o' paint . . . it hardly shows. . . ."

"How much were you expecting to get for it?" asked Mrs Venn, still gently.

"Twenty pounds," said the old lady, her eyes as sharp as black needles. "There was one of them on Arthur Negus. . . ."

Rachel gasped; the plate wasn't worth two; even *she* knew that. But Mrs Venn said, "Are you needing the money for something special . . .?"

"None of your business," said Mrs McNab, though her lips trembled more. She looked like she was going to break down and cry in the shop.

"I could give you five pounds," said Mrs Venn. "If that would help?"

"And you sell it for twenty? After it's been on Arthur Negus? You're sharks, you dealers. You're all the same . . . sharks." And she said it with real hate; and yet her lips were still trembling on the verge of tears. She grabbed her plate and fled. Suddenly, Rachel thought, Mrs Venn looked every year of her age; and weary with it.

And then suddenly she looked up and smiled, and twenty years dropped away. And Rachel became aware she wasn't the only looker-on in the shop. Dr Diggory was standing there, his raincoat open and splashed with dark rain, and his wet trilby hat in his hand. And he was smiling too; looking quite boyish and shy, in spite of his thinning hair and droopy little moustache.

"Trouble?" asked Dr Diggory.

"Trouble!" said Mrs Venn. They smiled again, together, and Rachel suddenly realised they were very good friends indeed. She'd hardly realised they knew each other . . . but she thought it was nice that two people she was so fond of should also be fond of each other. And how cosy to be with them, to overhear what they had to say. They might even speak about *her*, Rachel. Say how grown up she was getting, how intelligent, how fast she was learning about antiques.

But they didn't say anything to each other at first; just stood there staring silently, looking happier and happier, and younger and younger, till Rachel felt she would burst with happiness at such a miracle.

Then Dr Diggory said, "I've only got an hour . . . I have a surgery at six."

And Mrs Venn said, "Let's not waste it then. Go on through, then I'll make sure it's all clear and shut the shop. . . ."

"Waste?" thought Rachel. "Waste what? And why shut the shop?"

But Mrs Venn, suddenly businesslike and humming to herself with happiness, took her cashbox out of her desk and locked it, turned the card that hung in the door from "Open" to "Closed" and, with brisk flicks of the wrist, shot the bolts in the door, put out the shop lights, and vanished after Dr Diggory. Perhaps they're going to have tea, thought Rachel. If he's got surgery at six he'll need his tea. She'd often had tea with Mrs Venn herself. Toasted teacakes, home-made plum jam and Earl Grey tea, eaten in the deep chintz sitting-room chairs. So she still followed. . . .

But they didn't go into the sitting room. They were climbing the stairs, hand in hand, happy and chattering as a pair of schoolboys let out of school.

And the penny still didn't drop with Rachel. Dr Diggory was happily married; he had two grown up sons at university . . . perhaps Mrs Venn had bought some new treasure that she was working on upstairs in the boxroom and couldn't move . . . ?

But they didn't go into the boxroom; they paused by the open door of Mrs Venn's bedroom, and looked at each other with faces as radiant as angels.

Then they went in, and closed the door.

And Rachel knew where Mrs Venn's happiness came from, that she shared as willingly as a seat on a bus. . . .

And then she was back in the church, in front of the black spidery lettering that read,

THOU SHALT NOT COMMIT ADULTERY

She grew afraid, then. She had played three cards, and Zaphael had trumped them all.

All she had left was Daddy. She was so sure of Daddy; always kind, always patient, always with time to listen to her. But they had all been kind; Ziggy, Mrs Venn, Dr Diggory. They had all loved her and helped her. And had feet of clay.

She was still reeling under the shock of Ziggy; but Mrs Venn had overtaken Ziggy, like a big wave on the beach overtaking a smaller wave. And with Dr Diggory it was like two waves together. She felt like when you stand on the beach and the remains of those waves run back out to sea under your feet and you feel the whole beach is sliding away and you're afraid of falling. . . .

But Zaphael was cunning; she felt that. Broken and lost but cunning. Maybe he had pulled the trick in the antique shop to stop her trying Daddy at all. . . . She tried to imagine what Daddy's feet of clay might be . . . secret drinking like old Major Herbison, who tottered precariously about the village smelling of the mints he swallowed to hide the smell of alcohol?

Stupid. Daddy never tottered, or slurred his voice, and never smelt of anything but his old pipe. And smoking certainly wasn't in the Ten Commandments even if doctors did make a fuss about it . . . Daddy couldn't even be bothered to finish up the wine they had for dinner occasionally. Mummy always finished up his glass when she cleared the table.

Sex? She giggled. The women of the village watched Daddy like hawks, jealous if one old lady got ten minutes more visiting than another. It was a joke in the family. Certain old ladies always knew where Daddy was. If he was late home to lunch you only had to ring up one of them and ask her. No, Daddy was the most public person in the village . . .

She suddenly felt a traitor, sizing up Daddy's chances as if he was a racehorse she was going to bet on. . . .

So she walked straight up to the silent darkened Zaphael and said, "Daddy" with much more confidence than she really felt. She felt she was putting everything she owned on Daddy.

She was in the car, sitting where she'd always sat, on the back seat, peering out through the windscreen between

95

Mummy's and Daddy's heads. Through the windscreen, late afternoon sunlight was slanting across the trees and fields. Mummy was wearing her best suit, and that absurd hat she only wore for church occasions. Rachel knew it was today, and they were coming home from lunch with the Bishop.

And they were coming home in silence; from the distance they sat apart, from the stiff way they held their heads on their necks, the silence had been growing for some time. And that was bad.

She sat and sat, while the pretty black-and-white cottages of Frondsby passed and the rosegardens of Millborough, and the tarted-up watermill at Treesby. And still the silence continued. She watched Daddy's hands on the wheel and gearstick. The worse things got, the gentler his movements. Today his movements were very gentle indeed . . . the smell of the old car seat-leather made her feel sick.

Finally, on the long straight stretch that led into Munton, Mummy stirred, straightened in her seat and said,

"You're not going to *take* it, are you?" Her voice was full of contempt and that horrid near-certainty she used when she was trying to get things all her own way.

Daddy was silent still; if anything his hands were a little gentler as he changed down for a crossroads. Emboldened, Mummy went on,

"Being rural dean's an *old man's* job. It's a booby prize for also-rans . . . you wouldn't *want* it? You don't *want* it, surely?"

That was the point at which Rachel always gave in and said to her "Oh, all right Mummy, I don't *really* want it," and Mummy said approvingly, "Of course not – you've got far too much sense to want a thing like that." And Rachel would feel a great cloud of gloom descend, knowing that she'd wanted the thing very much indeed, and that now her chance of having it was gone for ever . . . so many things . . . the pilgrimage to Walsingham with the Youth Fellowship; the chance of riding lessons (so *bourgeois!*)

But Daddy still said nothing.

"Oh, so you *are* thinking of taking it? And then we shall see less of you than ever, I suppose? While you run about all over the county wiping the noses and backsides of silly young clergymen and middle-aged ones who should know better. . . . Well, don't ask me to lay on tea on the lawn for them all. I'm not running a café – I'll not be their bloody waitress."

"I have never asked you to do anything to help with my church work," said Daddy. It was, if anything, said in a lower softer voice than usual. But there was something in it that made Rachel shudder. A sound Mummy appeared not to hear.

"I should jolly well think not," she said.

"No," said Daddy, "I have left you free for much more important things, like criticising the Mother's Union and laughing at the WI and telling my churchwardens that they don't pay their farm-labourers enough . . . and going on demos about cruise missiles and appearing in court and getting your name in the local papers sailing paper boats down the river to commemorate Hiroshima."

"And so . .?" said Mummy defiantly.

"And slopping around in jeans you no longer have the figure for, and an anorak a farm-labourer's wife wouldn't be seen dead in, and moping around and playing the piano badly for days on end, when you can't even seem to see the washing piling up. . . ."

Mummy had heard the note in Daddy's voice too late; now she gave an audible gasp of pain, and seemed to slump as if wounded in her seat.

"And," said Daddy, "the level in the sherry bottle goes down and down, until suddenly there's a brand-new sherry bottle from the supermarket, and nothing for tea except beans on toast. And at that the toast will be burnt and the beans boiled out of their skins. And the house so smelly that the parishioners recommend cheap airsprays to me. . . ." His voice was still small and precise, like a surgeon's knife,

97

cutting. Mummy was starting to sob, her great tearing ugly childish sobs. But still the small voice went on and on, cutting, while the hands were still gentle on the steering wheel . . .

Take me out of here, thought Rachel. Please.

Zaphael must have heard. . . .

She stood before him, her head down, looking at the odd unearthly shapes of his brazen feet. Her mind searched endlessly for anyone else in the village who she could think of as good. She had tried a quick flick at the nice boy who delivered the milk, and had received in return from Zaphael a quick flick of that boy laughing over a bloody struggling rabbit in a snare. . . . She almost felt that Zaphael felt sorry for her . . . in her mind, she gave up, consented. Silently she asked, "When will you destroy the village?"

"AFTER THE CORN HARVEST."

She looked up at him swiftly, in surprise. The end of corn harvest was still three weeks off. Why should he wait so long?

It seemed to her that he wavered under her look; lost some of his massive bronze certainty.

"Why will you wait so long, Zaphael?"

Again that queer little wavering. She pressed in, and seemed to feel something yield.

"Why will you wait so long, Zaphael? You must tell me the truth, in the name of the Living God!"

"YOU WILL BE FAR AWAY THEN."

"You mean . . . while I am here you will not destroy it?"

The creature was still and silent. Something about its feel had changed. It felt different towards her . . . was it being sorry for her? But she took one look at the multi-eyed face, like the bronze face of a fly with leprosy, and knew that pity did not exist behind those many-faceted eyes. There had been no pity for Sodom and Gomorrah . . . no, it wasn't feeling pity; something else. Probing for weakness, she said,

"I shall not go away, Zaphael, ever. Then when will you destroy the village?"

"YOU MUST GO AWAY, IN OBEDIENCE TO YOUR FATHER."

She saw the trap in time. She was being tempted to break a commandment. Honour your father and your mother . . .

"Oh, I shall honour him, Zaphael. But I shall tell him honourably that I want to live at home and get a job. That I don't want to go back to school. I am old enough to leave school now." She added, "I shall never leave this village, while you are here, waiting to destroy it. I shall be trapped here, and you will be trapped here, till I die. Unless you choose to tell me you are going somewhere else."

She knew she had a grip on the creature now; it was like an immensely huge, immensely powerful dog, that she had outfaced. "What am I, Zaphael?" She knew she could never bring herself to say it, or even believe it. But she had to make *him* say it, for all their sakes.

"YOU ARE A RIGHTEOUS PERSON." She wanted to giggle, at the idea of *her* being righteous. But it was all to save the village.

"Where will you go, Zaphael?" She felt a touch of pity for him, now. "Cannot you go and find your friends?"

"I BELONG NOWHERE. ON THE DAY OF BATTLE, I WOULD NOT CHOOSE. I WOULD NOT CHOOSE MIKEL. I WOULD NOT CHOOSE SATAN. SO I MUST WANDER. . . ."

And then the church was suddenly quite empty. And the patch of sunlight on the floor of the chancel, that had been as steady as a searchlight all the time they had talked, developed the moving image of a cloud that passed across it and was gone. Then another cloud. She heard the wind sighing in the silver birch, and then it whistled round the buttresses of the tower. A strong draught blew in the open church door, carrying a pair of newly yellow autumn leaves.

Outside the world was unfrozen and moving again.

99

There was a double bang, from the pair of Phantoms from the US airbase. But it was softer; they were now flying very much higher.

She knew it was all over.

She walked out into her new lovely sinful kingdom.

A Nose Against the Glass

The town square at Beaminster is pleasant in summer. Always space to park a Mini, on the cobbles in front of the shops. In the middle, the warm stone of the market cross has, beneath its Victorian Gothic arches, seats where long-legged teenagers endlessly lounge and flirt. On Saturdays in August the morris men display their middle-class macho of ribbons, bells and sweat.

But that particular Christmas Eve it was deserted save for a few women, huddled and shapeless as Eskimos, flitting from shop to shop for the last few things. Dusk was coming early, with the big wet snowflakes that fell and died in the shining blackness of the Bridport road. The lights of passing cars caught them in a last flurry of incandescent glory as they died.

And in one corner of the square, old Widdowson sat in his gilded cage. It was really a large antique shop, painted Lapada-green with gilt lettering.

FINE ANTIQUES   T. F. WIDDOWSON   CLOCKS

But with its dim gold lighting from cunningly placed spotlights, with its flicker of brass on bezel and swinging pendulum, with the enduring patient stillness of the white-haired man sitting in one corner of the window, it did look, through the big falling flakes, like a gilded cage.

The passing women spared Widdowson a glance, a pang, a

timid wave. They knew he'd be alone this Christmas, as he'd been for the last ten. They remembered all his past kindnesses. Never refused to open a fête, old Widdowson; with a nice cheque to back it up. Never failed to give a small but exquisite object for the first prize in the Spastics Xmas Draw. But there was nothing they dared do for him; he was too rich, too dignified, too old. . . .

From his window, he missed none of this. Nothing wrong with his eyes and ears. They seemed to sharpen, as he grew older. So did his mind, when he might have welcomed a little merciful blurring round the edges. Nothing wrong with him at all, for eighty-four. People called him wonderful; said *they* wouldn't mind living to eighty-four, if they could be like Widdowson.

But they never said it to his face. . . .

The only thing wrong with Widdowson was the cold. Every summer, the sun seemed to lose a little more heart; every winter, the cold moved in a little closer. Oh, the shop was centrally heated; there was an extra fan-heater at his feet. People who came into the shop in overcoats and mufflers soon felt the prick of sweat. But Widdowson had learnt some time ago that this was not a cold that could be stopped by glass windows and thermostats. It seemed to him a cold within the earth itself; that reached up into the bones of his feet through the soles of his shoes; that came through the window-glass into his eyes, as the wet black road nudged towards freezing. Tonight in bed he would hear the cold, in the creaking of timbers and slates overhead; he would hear the crackle as ice-crystals formed. At this time of year the earth herself seemed close to death, despaired of the sun's return, could not succour those who lived on her.

Killing weather, he said to himself. Killing weather. He noted that Thomas, his black neutered tomcat, had crept silently into the warmest place in the shop, under the corner radiator, clear of any draughts. He was glad Thomas was home for the night, out of the killing weather . . . but he mustn't limit Thomas's freedom! He wasn't two yet, sleek and well-furred, with a lot of years before him. Widdowson had changed his will, last winter, to make sure Thomas would be properly cared for. Yet he remembered still the cat's skull he'd found as a boy on Morecambe beach; white and beautiful and perfect, but so small and thinly made. He could no longer rejoice in Thomas's thick-muscled wellbeing, without that skull being stamped across it, like a postmark cancelling out a bright postage-stamp.

Morbid. An old fool getting morbid. An old fool sitting here on Christmas Eve, waiting for customers who wouldn't come. Nobody bought antiques on Christmas Eve. Tinsel was what they were scurrying round looking for; packets of dates and cocktail-sticks. He could be sitting upstairs in comfort, with the curtains drawn and a new book, and the tray of tea Mrs Talbot had left him, with the kettle ready boiled. Alone, of course. Alone for the next four days. With the sweet smell of old men. Ever since he'd been a child, cuddled by his grandfather, he'd hated the sweet smell of old men. Now, it was always in his nostrils. Ten years ago he had first noticed it hanging about him. In a frenzy, he had bathed twice a day, changed his shirt three times, made a fool of himself with aftershave, till young girls looked at him and giggled. Now, he despaired; the smell of old men would be with him now till the end.

Someone might still come into the shop; nosiness would be his last pleasure to go. Like that elderly couple yesterday, both collectors. When the husband picked something up, on the point of buying, the wife said,

"Not now, dear. We must hurry. Elsie's waiting." And he would put it down again. Then the wife would pick up something else, and the husband would say,

"No time now, dear . . . Elsie's waiting." In the end they'd circled round for half an hour, jealous as cats, and gone away without buying, though they'd handled half the shop. Once, Widdowson would've been mad with chagrin, over a lost sale. Even ten years ago, he'd have felt sad for them, eternally denying one another's pleasure. Now he simply treasured them, as something as symmetrical and perfect as a Ming vase; popped them onto the shelves of his memory, to take down and dust and laugh over gently sometimes. While he could watch people he could drift through their lives painlessly, like an undemanding parasite. . . .

He glanced out of the window again. But in spite of the central heating, steam was condensing up the windows from the bottom sills like a subtle mist, cutting him off from the shop-lights across the road, making them look like the lights of ships sailing away out to sea. It made him feel he was going blind. He rubbed at the nearest pane angrily, with his fist and sleeve. Which only produced a jagged blear in which car-lights passed, distorted. A jagged blear like a calligraphy of impotent anger; as if he had written his pain on the window as clearly as the greengrocer next door wrote up the price of Brussels sprouts. For all the world to stare at.

The world had always stared; ever since he grew so tall and thin as a boy. He had always been careful to give them something else to stare at. Let them stare at his rows of grandfather clocks, every one a beauty, restored within and without until anyone might have thought they were brand-new from the hand of Knibb . . . he gave a lifetime guarantee on every clock. That had been a bold gesture when he first started as a young man. Wasn't worth much now. . . .

He looked at them, and they gave him no comfort; he thought they looked like big red highly polished tombstones. He grunted, either in disgust or pain. Fifty years serving clocks, saving clocks, pulling them back from the brink of ruin in the forties and fifties when fools chopped them up for firewood . . . and then the joy went out of it, like the tide going out at Morecambe Bay in his boyhood. They said he bought and sold them more shrewdly than ever; asked him still to verify the clocks at the antiques fair at Olympia. But it was only habit now; simply refusing to lie down. . . .

He turned again from the clocks to the window, like a driven thing. The mist of condensation had gathered again, mercifully erasing his angry calligraphy. All except one patch, little bigger than his hand.

And through that patch someone was staring in. A nose pressed against the glass, flat and white as a snail's belly. Two round blue eyes peering intently. Beyond the condensation's blur, a hint of pink lips and a fuzzy aureole that must be golden hair.

It made him jump. Then he had to laugh at himself for jumping. The face was so close to the pavement it could only be that of a child. A child staring in, in wonder, pussy-struck. And he knew somehow there was no harm in the child; it was not the sort who threw half-bricks through antique-shop windows, and certainly not the older sort of child that mugged elderly antique dealers and sometimes kicked them to death if enough money was not forthcoming. Which was as well for the child, for in the left-hand drawer of his desk was a Smith and Wesson of 1880, that might be antique, but was loaded with live ammunition. It might mean prison, even at the age of eighty-four. But prison was better than the humiliation of being mugged.

He looked again at the window, fleetingly, shyly. The child was still staring in, staring at *him* now. With what expression? Wonder? Amazement? Love? How absurd! But he stiffly managed a wink at the child; a grin, and finally a wave. But the blue eyes went on staring at him, unfathomable. How absurd, thought Widdowson, to stare at a relic like me in wonder. It is indecent! And in a sudden rush of embarrassment he waved the child away, not in anger so much as in panic. He knew the incredible wrinkles of his face too well from the shaving-mirror, and had never liked being stared at, even by the women he had loved.

The face vanished, leaving only darkness and the irregular metronome of car-lights.

And Widdowson allowed himself a rare lapse into

reverie; like his one cigar of the day . . .

That was how *he* had started, eighty years ago. Staring into the windows of junk-shops when his nose could hardly reach the sill. Like Ali Baba's caves they seemed then, the tangles of old bicycles, Chinese wood-carvings, fox-furs and engravings of the Old Queen, eyes hand-tinted blue and cold as the Arctic sky. His eye would explore further and further through the tangled jungle of wood and metal until it came to, at the back, silhouetted by the light of the rear-premises, the tall figure of the owner standing, staring back at him. Magicians they had seemed to him then; sellers of mystery, sellers of history who knew the origins of all things. That was why he'd always wanted to be an antique dealer. Now he was the best dealer in the south-west, he knew they had never been magicians, just dirty ignorant dishonest old men, desperately trying to scratch themselves a living sorting through the relics of the poor . . .

Suddenly he started up. What he needed was a stiff double whisky. Then he made himself sit down again. It was scarcely three o'clock in the afternoon. A double whisky now could be the start of the slippery slope. The one he'd slid down thirteen years ago, when Peggy died. The one he'd only just managed to climb out of. . . .

With the help of a nose pressed against the window.

Margie Harrison. Thin as a stick in a pair of threadbare jeans and a washed-out Rolling Stones tee-shirt, that at thirteen revealed a total lack of femininity. He'd been frightened, at first, of the young female thing who simply would not leave him alone. Any time of the day or evening he might look up to see her, tongue peeping out of the corner of her mouth, peering at the antiques with desperate longing. In the end he had tried to solve it by inviting her in to look round. That had been a mistake. Once in, she was almost impossible to get out. Questions, questions, questions. And that naïve way of asking "Is it gold? *Real* gold?" He had explained it was merely ormolu, bronze with gilding. That had been the beginning of the teaching. She had tried to repay with sturdy offers to dust, to make him a cup of tea. He dared not let her dust; she could do damage worth hundreds in ten minutes of misplaced vigour. He dared not let her go upstairs to make a cup of tea; she might be a cunning streetwise thief. But he could not bear to send her away; she was the only flickering candle in the drink-sodden dark of Peggy's death. So in the end he taught her to dust, and let her go and make the tea. And then, even as a widower of seventy-two, he grew terrified of village gossip, of being thought a dirty old man . . . he went to see her mother in the end, and had been welcomed. In that poor house any chance of work or money had been welcomed. It was agreed she would come and dust for him, after school and on Saturdays, for three pounds a week. And be taught the antiques trade. . . .

Three years it lasted. He taught her antiques, though she could never start to fathom the insides of a clock. He taught her how to speak properly, the meaning of the dealers' phrases, how to price an object. Until the incredible Saturday he had come back from delivering a long-case to find her so white and shaking he'd thought she'd been attacked. She could hardly speak . . . he'd had to shake it out of her. But no, it wasn't rape, it was a lady who had brought a pair of statues into the shop to sell. And she wouldn't wait . . . so Margie had bought them with forty pounds filched from the till . . . Widdowson had run through the shop to the back in a cold sweat. Forty pounds was forty pounds in those days.

But there in the back were a pair of Staffordshires, Victoria-and-Albert and Lord Nelson, genuine, filthy but unchipped, and worth at least a hundred pounds.

"Did I do right, Mr Widdowson? Did I do right?" Her soul was in her eyes, her open mouth. He had hugged her; he had given her another ten pounds out of the till as her commission; he had told her she'd make a real dealer some day. And in his heart, he had vowed to leave her the shop when he

107

died. That would shake them at the sales, cocky beggars. The first real woman dealer; in these parts anyway. He would start by taking her on full time, when she left school. . . .

Then, quite suddenly, it had all gone wrong. A boy called for her at the shop one night, a young soldier with a cocky jerky manner and a handsome bony white face. Barry Manson, who had the gift of dirtying things just by looking at them. He walked round the shop lifting all the price-tickets and whistling softly to himself. As they left together, as the door was closing, he heard the soldier say,

"You ought to ask for a raise; the old bugger's loaded."

He had been very patient, hoping it was a passing thing. She was used to handling things of quality now; surely she would see through Barry Manson. . . .

But she hadn't. A month later, shamefaced, she asked him for the raise. He gave it to her; he'd been meaning to, anyway. But it made him bitter; he felt he was giving the money to Manson. . . .

Of course he'd always known she would get married; she was an attractive girl, now, filling out. He'd hoped to give her away at her wedding, because her father had died by then. But he'd visualised something a lot better than Barry Manson. He'd hoped for a young auctioneer, or someone who came down regularly from Sotheby's. He'd looked forward to seeing her first child, perhaps being a godparent.

But not to Manson's child. A cloud grew between them; she still dusted well, and kept the shop with charm, but they didn't share their triumphs any more. He would catch her watching him, in mirrors, hurt, baffled, wondering what she'd done. But he could never bring himself to tell her. And when she said she was leaving school, he hadn't offered her the job. She'd gone to work in the gift shop instead, where they liked her ladylike ways. . . .

He sighed, and looked up at the window again, without thinking.

The eyes were back, peering in. So like her eyes. But not

her eyes, for she was still around. A big strapping woman, pushing a pram with Manson's third snotty-nosed child in it, going to fat a little more with each baby. Yet the eyes did have the same hurt locked-out look that hers had had, when she came to give notice before starting in the gift shop. . . .

A sudden impulse made him get up and go to the shop door. He did not know what he meant to say to the person outside.

So perhaps it was just as well there was nobody there. Just Mrs Peirson, locking up the greengrocer's next door. She turned and called, "Goodnight, Mr Widdowson. Merry Christmas!"

Curiosity drove him across to her. "Mrs Peirson? Have you just seen a child, peering in my window?"

"No, Mr Widdowson, I didn't see anybody. Mind you, I wasn't looking – a night like this. A child shouldn't be running about, a night like this . . ." She shivered, and he shivered in company. The snow was falling thicker, and lying now, at least on the pavements. Quite thick – an inch deep below his shop windows.

And then he saw. There were only three sets of footprints on the snowy pavement under his window. One set were his own; one set were large prints of a man in wellington boots; and the last were clearly a woman's.

Where the child should have stood, there were no prints at all.

Mrs Peirson, following his glance, gave him an odd look and said "Goodnight, Mr Widdowson," and hurried away.

He closed the door, and went back to his desk, shivering violently and not just with the cold. Was he going potty, like Walter Snowden had, and Violet Markham? He remembered the old people's home, Violet Markham's empty drooling face. . . . Please God, not that. Heart attack, stroke, cancer, anything but *that*. His mind was his strong fortress, his house of defence . . . even blindness he could have coped with, or deafness . . . but not to be himself, not to be in control of himself, to be a torn and whimpering rag of himself like Violet, or to go back to childhood like Walter . . . he would shoot himself first. He took the pistol from the drawer.

But it had an oddly soothing effect on him. It was not his destroyer, it was his child. *He* had bought it red with rust and broken. He had restored it till it gleamed subtly with the oil he had put on it. It clicked reassuringly in his hand. It worked perfectly, as he ejected the polished gleaming shells.

Was his mind working equally perfectly? He reached for his desk-diary, saw his appointments neatly inked in, all the way through to October next year. That wasn't a senile man's work. . . . One entry was merely pencilled in.

"Oatman – balloon-clock? £175?"

He reached for the phone and dialled Harry Oatman's number. Remembered it without having even to think. Harry's voice came down the phone, a little rough. Harry had started celebrating Christmas a little early. . . . A little cunning tiger wakened in Widdowson's mind. He might get the balloon-clock for a little less than £175 if Harry was fool enough to drink during business-hours. And Harry would be spent up, because he'd have given his feckless wife too much money to buy Xmas goodies. He'd *almost* promised to buy the balloon-clock, but not quite. He'd said he'd think about it . . . but Harry, with his silly optimism, would by now be considering the clock sold, and would have been spending accordingly. Widdowson's voice took on a croon of sad regret. Not too much – just a tinge of unhappy discomfort. . . .

"Harry, about that clock . . ."

He sensed Harry sensing the regret in his voice. And instantly panicking.

"*What* about that clock?" Harry tried to control his voice, but the panic showed through. Harry definitely had what he always euphemistically called a cash-flow problem. And if Widdowson didn't buy the clock, nobody else would, this side of New Year, when folk began spending their Christmas-

110

present money. And the bills would be flooding in, for the end of the year. . . .

"I don't think I can take that clock off you at the moment, Harry. I've just had one brought into the shop. A bit broken, but nothing I can't see to . . ."

A bit broken meant cheap.

"Look," said Harry, "I can see you right. A bit off . . ."

"How much off? I'm a little short of the ready myself."

"Will a hundred and sixty do you? Call it a Christmas present from me."

"You know I don't like stocking two balloon-clocks at once, Harry. Makes people think they're ten-a-penny. . . ."

"Look," said Harry desperately, "I'll be fair – after all, it is Christmas. Hundred and fifty to you, Widdowson. And that's a bargain. I won't take a penny less."

Which meant he would take more than a penny less.

"Hundred and forty," said Widdowson. The excitement of the chase filled his bloodstream like strong drink.

"Hundred and forty-five," said Harry weakly, seeing a glimmer of hope at the end of the long dark tunnel of Christmas.

"Done," said Widdowson. And, with the chase over, he not only felt flat; he felt he had been intolerably mean. Harry Oatman was a fool, but he had three kids, and it was Christmas. . . .

"Harry . . .?"

"Yeah?" The pain and worry of thirty lost quid was in Oatman's voice.

"That old wreck of a Victorian long-case – the one you've had for years – the one that's supposed to play tunes and doesn't. How much d'you want for it?"

"What you want *that* thing for?" Oatman's voice was incredulous with hope. The long-case had been stuck in his shop so long, so broken, it was the joke of the county.

"I feel like a problem to work on over the holiday. I think I can do it – if I can get the bats' nests out of it."

111

"If anybody can do it you can, Widdowson." Harry's voice was showing traces of maudlin admiration. "You can have it for a hundred."

"Ninety," said Widdowson sharply. He didn't want Oatman thinking he was going soft because it was Christmas.

"Ninety-five?"

"Ninety-five, then. When can you deliver?"

"Now if you like."

"Boxing Day will do. Boxing Day morning." He didn't want Oatman blundering through the snow with clocks in his present drunken state. Damn fool would probably get breathalysed.

"God bless you, Widdowson," said Oatman, now thoroughly maudlin. "You're a good bloke. My missus–"

"Must go, Harry," said Widdowson crisply. "Merry Christmas." He hung up; he could never stand being thanked.

He felt better. He felt like a cat who has played with a mouse and mercifully let it go. And he knew he'd lost none of his old edge.

Senile? Rubbish!

He looked up.

The eyes were watching through the window again. Beseeching.

Again he ran to the door. Again there was no one there, and no footprints in the snow. But the snow was falling very fast now. All the world was white for Christmas, and the lights of the shops across the square were hardly visible through the black falling flakes; as he watched, another shop window went dark. Only three left now – the gift shop where Margie had worked, the Post Office and the Dumbledore Cafe. Not a soul was in sight; the scurrying housewives had all collected their Christmas store.

Widdowson felt suddenly, bleakly, alone.

He looked across the narrow street that led out of the village towards Crewkerne. Across the road the restaurant

112

still had its lights on, was still serving afternoon tea.

He hadn't been inside for years. But it looked just the same, warmly red with its undrawn curtains, and a little lamp on each table, shining on silverplate and knapkins.

He decided tea would be better than a whisky.

Close to, Sheila Watkins who ran it was just the same; a little plumper, a little more lined, a few more grey hairs, but the last ten years hadn't levied too sharp a price. She still bubbled with excitement, as she had when she was a plump schoolgirl, indulging herself in a treat at one of the same tables she now owned. . . .

"Mr Widdowson – how *nice*! I think we've got your usual table vacant for you!" Widdowson appreciated her gift of salesmanship. He hadn't been in the place for ten years. And indeed she had remembered his favourite table, back to the wall in the far corner, with a view over the square at his shoulder so he could keep an eye on everything, like a fading gunfighter in an old Western.

"Tea? Toasted teacakes?" She had remembered his liking for teacakes, too. She probably remembered he liked them well done, slightly black on the very edges. A surge of warmth swept over him. She was a comfortable sort of woman, even in her widowhood. The sort any decent man could safely marry, if she'd have him. He'd toyed with the idea of asking her, after Peggy died . . . but women were vulnerable creatures, prone to cancer in middle-age, and he couldn't have borne to be hurt again.

"Teacakes," he said, to make up for not proposing to her twelve years ago. She went and gave his order, then came back, beaming. "Can you spare a moment, Mr Widdowson – while they're toasting. I . . . I've bought a clock I'd like you to see. Of course it's not like *your* clocks . . . but I think it's rather nice." She sighed comfortably. "When I saw it, I couldn't resist it."

She led him upstairs, across a landing that smelt pleasingly

113

of polish, He felt a twinge of delightful guilt, imagining for a moment he was her lover . . . then he was laughing at himself for being an old fool.

Her sitting room was as comfortable as she was, plump chintz and a smell of pot-pourri. He got a sense of her hidden life; there were two books on the table by the settee. *Hawksmoor* by Peter Ackroyd, and *Life in the English Country House* by Mark Girouard. The lady was no fool. . . .

"Here's my clock." She paused and gestured, half-proud, half self-indulgent.

The clock hung on the wall, neatly lit by a spotlight. It was a reproduction of a Dutch wall-clock, with hanging brass weights and a crudely filed brass figure of Atlas holding up the world. It was perfectly *horrible*; expensive and vulgar, a travesty to anyone who'd ever seen a real Dutch clock. He had to stop himself gritting his teeth and closing his eyes in agony. He could have got her a genuine, honest mahogany schoolroom clock for the price she'd paid. If only she'd come to him. . . .

But she was waiting for his opinion, eyes shining and mouth a little open, still looking like a schoolgirl, in spite of over-white false teeth. Expectant eyes again. . . . And she had made him welcome, and it was Christmas. . . .

He said, still clinging desperately to his honour.

"Yes – a Dutch clock. I've seen them in The Hague. The old ones are rather bigger. . . ."

But she would not let him off the hook. "But do you like it, Mr Widdowson? Do you *approve*?"

He forced the lies out, as if he was being sick.

"I think it's very nice, Mrs Watkins. Remarkable. Very sound craftsmanship."

"Well, that coming from you is a *real* compliment." Now she would be telling everybody in town what he'd said. People would be laughing at him behind his back. Thank you, Mrs Watkins. You've just extracted my lifetime-earned good name as your Christmas present. Merry Christmas!

114

But he'd still like to have sat down on her chintz couch, have her fetch him a cup of tea and fuss over him; sit by the cosy log fire and warm his feet. He was weary; women gave warmth and food and love; all they demanded in exchange was your integrity. . . .

"Yes, very nice," he said again, and trailed off.

"Your teacakes will be ready by now," she said.

But he revived, downstairs. George McLoughlin came across to wish him a Merry Christmas, and show off his grandfather's golden hunter watch, which could truthfully be admired. Ken Smith, who he hadn't seen for ten years since he moved to Bridport, clapped him on the shoulder patronisingly, and told him he didn't look a year older. He wryly consoled himself that Ken Smith looked a great deal older; he had halved his hair and doubled his waistline. A sort of little court gathered around him, hanging on his every word, as if he was minor royalty. And the teacakes were unusually good and dripping with butter. . . .

But it was the girl across the room who caught his eye. A tall slim elegant girl, carelessly but stylishly dressed. Not a local Dorset dumpling. She was with a plump young man, of a sort that Widdowson did not like; a type he seemed to see more and more. Young Tories he called them, as opposed to old Tories. Always talking about how much money they were making. Always going a bit to fat, far too young. Too many expense-account lunches. Spotty faces and sharp Italian suits and camel overcoats . . . vulgar. Always in accountancy and city banking . . . no breeding. This one was holding forth on money now; and calling Cabinet Ministers by their Christian names. Norman and Leon and Nigel. . . . Sickening.

Girl wasn't very impressed either. Sexy bit – she had her legs crossed and was letting her shoe hang away from her heel. Widdowson had always taken that as a sign a woman was hunting for a man . . . nice naked heel, in its silk stocking, nice elegant leg. But she wasn't much pleased with the man she'd caught this time. . . . As he talked she was

drawing little squares in the air with her dangling foot . . .
sure sign of boredom.

And sensitive; she became aware he was watching her.
Turned to look at Widdowson; he liked the long elegant nose
and the huge brown eyes. For a moment she looked at him as
if he was a real person, not some old gaffer to be immediately
discounted.

Delicately, wickedly, Widdowson glanced at her young
man's averted head, and sketched a little pound-sign in the
air with his finger, and grinned conspiratorially.

She *was* sharp: she got it; she laughed out loud. Just for one
glorious moment he was her brilliant and wicked grandfather. Then the young man turned and scowled at him,
thunderously. A low-voiced row seemed to be breaking out
between them. Then she was standing up and gathering her
belongings . . .

As she swept past, he looked up a little timidly, a little
appalled at what he'd done.

She gave him a wink, and a wide smile. For a blinding
second, sixty years of age between them didn't matter. Then
she was gone, leaving a hint of perfume that might have been
Chanel Number Five, or didn't they make that any more?
Then the young man was blundering after her. If looks
could've killed. . . . Widdowson met his eyes steadily, and
the young man looked away first . . . but then, Widdowson
told himself fairly, the young man had to look where he was
going. . . . As it was, he blundered into a table and knocked a
chair over. Didn't stop to pick it up, either; threw money onto
the counter to pay his bill and didn't wait for the change.

"Rudeness," said Sheila Watkins stoutly at his retreating
back. "Well, he needn't bother coming here again. I can do
without his kind of business."

And Widdowson was left with his Pyrrhic victory. If only
he'd not interfered, he might have had another ten minutes
to watch the girl. Still, he wished her luck with her life. She
might know heartbreak – who didn't, sooner or later – but

even as an old woman, she'd have style.

The restaurant, without her glow, turned as bleak as a black-and-white movie. Widdowson sniffed in the air deep, like an old hound hunting for fox-scent. But all trace of the Chanel Number Five had vanished. She had sailed away like a glorious ship, laden with life and love and giggles and excitement and the sheer young health that surged in her from morning till night.

And he was left on the quayside, waving hopelessly. I would give the shop and the clocks and my bank balance and everything I own, he thought, to shed sixty years and run down the street after her, in rags. He had no doubts about his power to attract her, even in rags. . . .

He poured himself another cup of tea, to cheer himself up; listened to a man trying to sell another man a car. The man was too quick and jumpy, too pushy . . . he failed to sell his car. Bad salesman, serve him right, thought Widdowson. He went and paid his bill in restored good-humour, working out how *he* would have sold the car . . .

Mrs Watkins told the coroner later that Mr Widdowson left her restaurant in apparently the best of health and spirits. She was the last person who really saw him alive. . . .

The cold seemed to have got into the shop like a burglar while he was away. Thomas kept getting up and circling round as if trying to find a warmer arrangement under the radiator. Widdowson suddenly felt tired; he crawled behind his desk as if it was a refuge. It would have been wiser to go upstairs, where the windows were curtained against the frost; but he didn't feel up to the stairs yet.

The idea of starting all over again would not go away. He had exchanged his youth and strength for a lot of money. He was *still* making a lot of money. Now he no longer cared, everything he touched seemed to turn to gold; he could make a thousand pounds in a fit of abstraction; like the last auction

117

he'd been to, at Sotheby's. Bidding for a huge funny-looking clock that nobody seemed to know much about that had mildly pricked his curiosity because it was covered with domes and minarets, though it had a French movement and a lot of seized-up works that must make a very funny noise indeed when they were freed of verdigris and actually functioning. He'd wanted it to fiddle with, really, in the long dark evenings. Anyway, he had gone on bidding, languidly waving his hand and listening with half an ear to the rising price, to make sure he didn't pay more than it was worth, and all the time thinking about that last summer holiday he'd had in Normandy with Peggy.

He'd come to with a start, hearing the voice of the auctioneer knocking the clock down to him for five hundred and fifty. The next second he had been accosted by a tiny man in a business suit and a djellabah. Obviously an Arab, though he spoke good English in spite of his panic, and spat saliva all over Widdowson's lapels. He had made so much fuss, the auctioneer had three times called for silence before he began the next lot.

The little man was really very upset indeed. Widdowson, amidst stares, had led him out into the foyer, and managed to calm him down and get his story.

The clock was a French clock, made for the Mahommedan Middle East market, in the middle of the nineteenth century. It had been sold to the Sultan's ancestor, but mislaid during some palace insurrection in about 1920. The present Sultan had just heard of the clock's existence while on a trip to London. He had sent his aide-de-camp to bid, but the aide-de-camp had had a hard time finding a taxi, got stuck in several traffic-jams, had trouble establishing his master's credit with the auctioneer's clerk, and heard the clock knocked down as he entered the room. . . . The aide-de-camp's face was working pitifully; his master's instructions had been to buy the clock at *any* price, and not return without it. The aide-de-camp dare not return without it; reduction to the rank of camel-driver was the least of the punishments he feared. . . .

Widdowson had felt sorry for the little man, with his beaky nose and large dark tear-filled eyes. He pitied any man who worked for the powerful. He had put his arm on the shoulder of the rather absurd brown pin-stripe suit; and promised to sell the clock to the master . . . at double the price, of course, and only after he, Widdowson, had restored it to perfection from its present sorry condition . . . which would cost at least another five hundred. Perhaps they had better collect the clock and pay for it, and go and see the master together. . . .

That had been quite an evening. Eastern hospitality was all it had ever been cracked up to be, and Arab princes really were charming people when they got their own way. Later, the Sultan had arrived at the shop in person to collect his ancestor's clock. In a brand-new white Rolls-Royce that had parked on the double yellow lines, and given the village of Beaminster something to gossip over for weeks. . . . But after the Sultan had finally gone, there was only an entry for £1500 in Widdow-. son's bank statement, which seemed to get more meaningless, the more it filled up with noughts and commas. . . .

That was the worst of it. All the excitement of the hunt; all the love in restoring the clock; and then the flatness of the bank statement. A thousand pounds, ten thousand pounds, could make no difference to him now.

Anyhow, he'd never been looking for money (though he'd hated being without any). He'd been looking for . . . the pearl of great price. He had to admit it, old fool that he was. All his life he'd been looking for the pearl of great price. All through the enforced church-attendances of his boyhood, that had been the one Bible-reading that had made sense. The merchant who'd sold all to buy the pearl of great price. The one feller in all that religious nonsense that had been a solid believable human being. The excitement of selling all that you had. For the ultimate. . . .

He'd never found the pearl. Oh, there was the Chippendale

119

commode he'd mortgaged the shop for. He'd nearly lost the shop, while Sotheby's New York were waiting to sell it, and all the so-called experts were doubting its provenance. . . . There was the Tompion long-case that took every penny in his pocket as a young man. There was the life-sized bronze of Kuan-yin the Buddhist Bodhisattva, that still stood across the shop from him; that was as good as the one in the British Museum, and nearly as good company now as Thomas the cat. He looked across at her, with great affection; the full bronze breasts exposed, confident and sensuous, above the long skirt; the dreaming face above; she was mistress of herself, in the world of flesh as well as the world of spirit. He had sat hours staring at that dreaming face, while he waited for word from the hospital about Peggy. He had found the cold comfort of beauty in her; as he had found it in his first Chinese woodcarving, bought at seventeen, while he listened to his father's drunken shouting, his mother's acid screaming, coming up through the ceiling into his bedroom.

Beauty was a cold comfort in trouble. But it was a sure small comfort that nothing could take away. . . .

But there was no ultimate beauty; no pearl of great price worth not less than everything.

Again, he looked at the strange patch in the steam of the window; looked at it now almost as if it was an old friend.

He would have been disappointed if the eyes had not been there. . . . He was no longer afraid of them; or afraid for his own sanity. He accepted them as part of him now; as he accepted his wrinkles and the slight ache of rheumatism in his right hip when the weather was cold.

He looked at the blue eyes straight. Accepted their yearning. He knew those eyes too were looking for the pearl of great price, one each side of the nose pressed like a snail's belly against the window. He wondered, half-numb with cold, if the eyes were those of his own infant self. He looked at the eyes sadly and shook his head.

120

"Go on, then, look. Go on looking. But I tell you, young man, it's a snare and delusion. There is no pearl of great price. Why don't you go off and have fun, instead, while you can? Go and get warm! Grow up and find a good woman, and go to bed with her as often as you can. . . ." Maudlin old bugger, he thought, a maudlin old bugger talking to himself.

But to his great amazement, the eyes responded. They moved rapidly from side to side of the bare patch.

The child outside was shaking its head; very emphatically. The child outside was insisting there *was* a pearl of great price.

"All right," he said to the eyes, which were now still and watching him intently again. "Have it your way; it's your life."

Again, through the steamy glass, the child shook its head vigorously. For some reason, Widdowson became convinced the eyes would not run away this time; it was worth the effort of going to the shop door once more. He almost tiptoed across to it; he kept on looking across to the patch, to see if the eyes had vanished. But they didn't.

He swung open the shop door; heard the shop-bell clang above his head. Took a step outside, a big swift step; and felt the thickening snow slide treacherously under his feet. So he finally went out onto the pavement with a rush and slither. When he'd recovered his balance, he looked up.

The child was still standing there; it was smaller than he thought. But, and he gasped in horror, it was only wearing some thin threadbare nightgown thing that didn't come down to its bare knees.

And the small thin feet were bare upon the snow.

An icy gust of wind came round the corner, ruffling the child's nightgown; it was so cold it tore right through Widdowson's sheepskin coat and thick polo-neck sweater. He thought with anguish, closing his eyes against it, how cold the child must be. Then he opened his eyes, hoping the child was only a figment of his imagination, and would have vanished.

121

But it was still standing there, looking at him. He noticed how thin its legs were; the feet were almost transparent against the snow; he could see their blue veins and thin ankle-bones standing out. The arms below the short sleeves were like sticks. The face was huge-eyed, hollowcheeked. The stomach was large, swollen with hunger. The face seemed to be bruised down one side. And yet still the child looked beautiful. He remembered the newsreels from Ethiopia; he remembered how the children there still had this way of looking beautiful, even when they were dying. . . .

But this wasn't an Ethiopian child; it was fair long hair that whipped in the cruel wind; the huge eyes were blue, like his own.

A terrible sense of disorder filled Widdowson; it was impossible that any *English* child should be in this state; any *Beaminster* child. What were the teachers doing . . . the social workers from Bridport? He became incoherent with the outrage of it . . . but then there had been stories in the papers about English children. But not in Beaminster. Everybody knew everybody's business in Beaminster.

Then he snatched himself back to looking at the child. To thinking straight. Perhaps the child was a Christmas ghost from long ago. From the hungry forties, the eighteen-forties. Children must have starved in Beaminster *then* . . . under the Corn Laws and the Speenhamland system. After all, the child had left no footprints outside his window.

But now the child put one pale bony foot forward, then took it back again. And Widdowson could see, quite clearly, a five-toed footprint in the snow. It was a real child. It was telling him it was a real child.

He moved towards it, his arms outstretched, mumbling incoherently about coming into the warm, having food. He heard himself mumbling something about milk and biscuits . . . Christmas cake.

The child began to back away from him.

Then it turned and ran. Vanished round the corner. . . .
Two cars passed Widdowson in rapid succession, their
headlights showing snowflakes as big as goose-feathers,
reminding him of that childhood nursery rhyme.

He looked back into his shop. The door was swinging
wildly in the gusts of wind, where he had left it open. Flakes
of snow were falling inside the shop onto the fitted carpet,
melting to damp dark spots. The papers were blowing off his
desk, the smaller pictures fluttering on the wall. He saw
Thomas's tail, fleeing up the stairs. He even thought he saw
one of the taller, thinner clocks sway . . . impending chaos.
And another searing gust of wind tore into him, making him
gasp and nearly knocking him off his feet. He felt, with all his
eighty-four years, how frail the human body is.

He must get back into the shop and get the door shut. The
temperature in there must be dropping like a stone, the
humidity going up . . . damp was bad for clock-veneer. Cold
blowing up the stairs, invading his living-quarters . . . it
would take the central-heating all evening to get it back to
normal. Once back inside, he could ring the police about the
child. Teddy Hollings, the local constable was Beaminster
born and bred. He'd know every nook and cranny. He'd
know how to contact the Social Services.

He got back inside and forced the door shut, and sat at his
desk. He made a feeble attempt to pick his papers off the
floor, but the effort to bend made his head swim. Besides, he
must dial the local police station. He was a long time doing it;
his fingers felt like frozen sausages.

Finally, he got through. Mrs Hollings. Teddy wasn't in;
there'd been a serious pile-up near the tunnel on the
Crewkerne Road; people hurt. The ambulance was being
slow in getting through. It could take hours to clear. The
nearest available panda was back in Bridport. . . .

He hung up in despair. No help there tonight. He rang the
Social Services number; it was already on Answerphone;
gave a Dorchester number to ring for the duty officer. What

the hell would Dorchester know about finding a child in the alleyways of Beaminster?

He looked out of his window, across the square; the last of the shop-lights had gone out. He looked at his watch. Of course, it was nearly six o'clock. Normally his own lights would be off; only the dim security-lights would be left on. Even the restaurant-lights were off; Sheila Watkins wouldn't open again on Christmas Eve; everyone was home with their families, getting ready for Christmas; the poorest night in the year for dining-out, she always said. He rang her upstairs flat anyway; but she didn't reply. She had probably gone to stay with friends. Hardly anybody else lived over the shops round the square. Nobody who he'd care to tell about a child in a nightgown; they'd think he was drunk and babbling. . . .

The thought of a drink was like manna in the wilderness. He went to the cabinet, in the office at the back of the shop, where he kept a few choice bottles for extra-special customers. Poured himself a large whisky, infuriated at the way his shaking hands spilled it on the leather top of the desk. He was so cold, cold. . . .

Not as cold as the child. Not dying of cold, like the child must be. Why the hell didn't it have the sense to go home to the warm? Then he remembered the bruise on its face. Perhaps it didn't go home because it was frightened of being beaten? Battered? Murdered?

He paced up and down the shop, whether to get warm or to work off his anxiety even he couldn't tell. He stopped every five paces to gulp more whisky, feeling it dribbling down his chin. The windows were all steamed up now; the hole the child had stared through was gone. It was, to his coward self, a source of relief. It kept the child . . . outside. He didn't have to see it any more. After all, he'd offered to have it in, get it warm, feed it, find it help. If the silly little thing had run away from him, was it *his* fault? He'd done what he could . . . risked his life. He'd nearly fallen; and at his age, a fall often meant a broken hip, and a broken hip

124

usually meant the end. There was no point in them *both* dying . . . You couldn't expect a man of eighty-four . . .

And then the weeping started. Right outside the window. A weeping that would have broken anybody's heart. As if all the world was weeping.

He forgot everything. He ran to the door and ran out into the snow. He almost caught the child; one second his arms were closing round it, and the next his foot had slipped and it was gone out of his arms.

It ran across the square to the shelter of the Market Cross, where the teenagers lounged in summer. No shelter there tonight; the wind would be howling through the four Gothic arches . . . but he could see it underneath those arches by the lamplight that filtered dimly, through the snowflakes, from the few streetlamps. It was only a dim flicker of white nightgown and golden hair blowing in the wind, but he knew somehow the shadowed blue eyes were still watching him. Perhaps it would talk to him on its own ground.

He gathered his strength and ran. There was a sudden flare of headlights, a blare of horn, the long screech of tyres on packed snow, and something large and dark missed him by inches; he felt the size, the weight of it in the wind of its passing, and the eddies it caused in the snowflakes. The driver later told the coroner he'd seen this old white-haired gaffer running like the wind. But he was sure he hadn't hit him; quite sure.

Widdowson had shot his bolt by the time he reached the cross; he felt the snow which had dropped inside his shoes start to melt; he felt his old lungs creaking like bellows. He knew he was spending more strength than he had, and he'd never overspent his strength in his life. Fool, said a voice in his head, a voice whose sense he'd always trusted in the heat of the hottest auction. Fool, go back, before it's too late.

But the child was gone from the cross; Widdowson thought he'd vanished altogether, till he saw a flicker of blowing gold in the gutter outside the gift shop. The child was lying in the gutter, motionless . . . unconscious? Lamed by the fall? In any case, he'd be no bother now. . . .

Widdowson ran on at half-speed; well, a fast totter really, he thought with a grim flick of humour. He pulled up in a heart-rending skid, just kept his feet, and reached down to pick up the child . . .

. . . who catapulted from between his outstretched hands like an untamed cat, and was running away down the road towards the church. Then slipped and fell again, as it reached the corner, and again lay still. Was it injured in some way, concussed? Or was it playing up? Funny thing, playing up, if it meant lying on the freezing snow in a nightgown. But if it was concussion, which would fit in with the bruise on the face, it might mean the child *couldn't* get up again; might lie in the snow and freeze to death like a new-born lamb. He *must* get to it. The slope down to the church was steep and treacherous; he hadn't even brought a stick, which he usually carried when the road was slippery. He made progress slowly now, clinging on to whatever he could, drainpipes, window-sills. He crept past the windows of the other antique shop, and noticed she had a bronze Chinese vase with cloisonné enamel in her darkened window, which at £55 was definitely undervalued. Funny how bits of your mind worked on their own, in the most ridiculous circumstances. . . .

Behind him, his shop door was blowing in the wind again, his papers scattering, his pictures fluttering, a clock, taller and thinner than the rest, rocking. No burglar alarms were set. Had certain gentlemen well-known to Scotland Yard's Fine Art squad passed that way with a furniture-van that night, they could have helped themselves to stuff worth a quarter of a million . . . but it was an hour before anybody noticed. Teddy Hollings, returning exhausted but thankful from the road-traffic incident at the tunnel, was still alert enough to stare aghast and nearly crash his own car. He searched the ground floor, and found nothing but weather

126

damage, though the fluttering sheets of paper blew around the shop like birds, and whispered like ghosts. He went upstairs, fearing to find the worst, and found nothing. He reported the incident in to headquarters, and thought about a search . . . but search where?

Widdowson made the journey to the bottom of the hill with his head down all the way, placing every foot with infinite care, fighting for his life as a younger man might have fought on Everest. From the various houses came little bursts and squeaks of Christmas noise. Children shouting and laughing; a record-player playing 'Silent Night', which Widdowson had come to dislike more than any TV jingle, through the sheer amount of repetition. He could have called for help, but he was too proud and stubborn, and he knew if he met anyone he was too shaken to talk coherently. He had a terror of not being coherent. . . .

When he reached the bottom of the hill, the child was gone. He might have thought himself deluded, but he could see where the child's body had dented the snow, and a trail of naked tiny footprints, leading uphill now to where the church tower bulked black and huge above the mounded snow. There was a haloed moon behind the black flakes of falling snow, and by its light he thought he could see something white flicker in the church porch. Moaning to himself, clinging to the rough wall of the churchyard, he climbed up hand over hand, past the wrought-iron gates that stood open ready for Midnight Mass, and into the porch.

The porch was empty; only the notices fluttering like sleepy restless white hens on the notice board. But he was glad to reach it; it was quiet and warmer, out of the wind. And the door into the church was a little open . . . Aha, he thought. Got you! He pushed the creaking door open, went in, closed it with an effort behind him, and locked it with the key and put the key in his pocket. You won't get away from me now, my lad!

The church was dark, but very warm. They must be warming it up ready for Midnight Mass. It would be a help if he could put the lights on, but he hadn't been in the church for thirteen years, since he buried Peggy. And forty years before that, when he married Peggy. Would the switches be by the door, which was logical; or would they be somewhere up by the pulpit and organ? There was a little light coming in now, through the huge dark-blue windows. It bounced and flickered on the tops of the pews; and the east window showed the light of one streetlamp through its stained-glass; enough to outline the rood-screen and the cross fixed above it. Beautiful black pattern. And the glowing tiny red light above the altar . . . But of switches he could see no sign, as he groped from pew-top to pew-top, afraid of falling over something hidden by the darkness of the floor.

Very well. If there were no switches, if he couldn't see, he must listen. He sat down heavily in the front pew; and was grateful that the ache in his legs eased. He took out his handkerchief, and wiped the damp that melting snowflakes had left on his face; brushed the thick snow off his coat and trousers . . . then he settled to listen. His ears seemed extra-acute now. He turned his head this way and that, listening to every sound. And found the church full of sound; the creaking of rafters and pews as the church warmed up. Noises from outside, voices, the sound of a bicycle free-wheel, oddly distorted and magnified.

After a while he became convinced the child was there; he could sense it waiting in the dark, listening with equal intentness.

"Boy?" he called, with some authority, now he had got his breath back. "Boy? Come here, boy! I won't hurt you!" He tried to make his voice gentler and gentler, as you would with a timid or abused animal; he had always been good at making friends with animals. Then, as nothing happened, he would grow cross, try to command the boy. Then he would grow ashamed of his own self-defeating anger, and make his voice soft again.

128

And all the time he felt the child watching, drawing nearer. . . .

But it was still a terrible shock when he saw the child standing at the foot of the chancel steps, only about six feet away, and quite still. And Widdowson knew with equal shock that the child was no longer afraid. The child seemed utterly at home here . . . so that it was Widdowson who grew a little afraid of the child's surety and stillness. But he said, with a gruff bravery he did not feel, "Well, you have led me a dance! What're you doing out on a night like this? We're going to have to get you sorted out!"

Still the child neither spoke nor moved. And Widdowson hardly dared to speak to it again; he might have the church key in his pocket, but he knew he was the prisoner now. Not that he much cared; it was so warm in the church, and his legs had stopped hurting. He felt himself dropping into a cosy doze; and leapt back awake, thinking this would never do. People coming into church for Midnight Mass might find him snoring, with his mouth open, like some old tramp that had crept in out of the wind. He made a last effort. An attempted joke.

"Looking for the pearl of great price, were you? Well, you'll not find it in my shop."

But the child slowly shook its head. As if to say he would.

"I don't know where, then, boy. I've been looking for it myself, for eighty years, and *I've* not found it."

The child raised its hands in a gesture towards Widdowson, as if offering him something. As if offering Widdowson Widdowson himself.

Widdowson laughed; a frighteningly creaky laugh, as if his lungs were going off-duty. "What, an old wreck like me? You'd find better in Thompson's second-hand shop."

But the child shook its head again. With the utmost surety. So that Widdowson cried out in panic.

"Who are you, boy?"

The child raised its hands again, fully open now.

129

Widdowson could see dark dribbling marks, in the centre of each wrist. . . .

Widdowson remembered what night it was, and was flatly and unquestioningly satisfied. He began to fall asleep.

But there was one thing he must do. Must write. He fumbled in his pockets and after a long while found a Biro. There were carol sheets glimmering whitely all along the pew, laid out for Midnight Mass.

He just managed to finish writing.

It was a great shock for the churchwardens when they arrived. The door locked unexpectedly, when they were sure they'd left it open, ready. They had to send to the verger for the spare key. And when they put the lights on, there was this man sitting in the front pew. A man who'd been inexplicably sitting in the dark. They called out to him; he did not reply. . . .

"Looks like old Widdowson!"

"Never seen *him* in church before!"

But they were trembling as they walked up to him.

"Mr Widdowson!"

"He's dropped off!"

They shook him gently. The awful coldness of his face told them he was dead.

He just sat staring; staring at the wooden angel that held up the lectern and the Bible; an angel with a white-painted robe and long golden hair; it was about four feet tall; about the size of a child, with upraised hands to support the Bible above its head. . . .

"Good God!"

"He's . . . smiling."

"Grimacing . . . musta been his heart."

"Poor old bugger, he was a good age."

"About eighty-five."

"Not a bad innings . . ."

"I'm glad the women didn't walk in and find him. Go and

ring the police. I'll keep the women out of church. Enough to ruin their Christmas. Here . . . what's this? He's written something."

"Don't touch it. Leave it for the coroner."

"It's not a suicide note – it's a sort of will."

About my money – give it all to the children. Signed, T. F. Widdowson

"Not much of a will – that won't stand up in court. Not witnessed, is it?"

"And I bet he's left a packet, too. Go on, go and ring the police. I'll stay with him."

Terence Fairfax Widdowson was found by the coroner to have died from a massive infarction of the heart, probably brought on by undue exertion.

The will he left in the church was not granted probate, lacking any witnesses that he was "of sound testamentary disposition". His earlier will prevailed. Thomas the cat has been well looked after, but finds it difficult to find a draught-free spot to settle in his new home.

The antiques business was sold as a going concern; it still has Widdowson's name over the door; but a new man sits in the gilded cage.

Author's note

I apologise to the antique dealer of Beaminster, whose shop, complete in every detail, I have borrowed for this story. I know nothing of the real owner except that he or she sells very good clocks.

RAW

Artist on Aramor

If you want to see a magic sight, go to Bridport in August. Look along the main street at sunset. Watch the red circle of the declining sun sink towards the half-circle of the town hall dome. At the far end of the street rises a breastlike hill with a ringed nipple of trees. The strings of carnival flags, criss-crossing the street, make half-circles too. It is almost as if the sun is settling into a bed of them, all lost in a mist of purple and gold and sun-blinding haze.

The sun dropped behind the nippled hill, and I bent and washed out my brushes in the paraffin-bucket. I could hardly see down there in the shadows, because my eyes were still full of sunset, and everywhere I looked there was a dark green ring in the centre of my vision, where the sun had temporarily blinded me. Even when I looked back at my canvas, the green ring was there, leaping about the painted surface as I blinked. But it was fading. More important, I'd *got* it; after near-blinding myself for twenty sunsets, I'd captured that magic moment that only Bridport has. Still rough and dribbly, but from now on it was only a matter of tidying up.

There was a knock on the door. Mrs Greaves' querulous voice.

"Mr Martell, there's one of them green fellers here to see you. I made him wait till you were finished." She knew the meaning of my every movement, as some housekeepers do,

132

right down to the rattle of paintbrushes in a galvanised iron bucket.

I wiped and washed my hands, dried them on the painty towel that was her despair, and went down.

It was a green feller indeed; and as is the way with green fellers, he'd helped himself to my whisky, uninvited. He was a fine specimen, green and shiny as a rhododendron leaf, with that skin that wrinkles too easily for human taste. He had the usual Hanoverian profile, receding forehead beneath receding hair, a massive and imperious nose, rubbery sensuous lips, and no chin worth mentioning. He was wearing the usual hand-made silk shirt, and probably silk underwear too; they cannot bear anything rougher next to that shiny wrinkled skin of theirs. His suit was cut in Savile Row from the look of it; in fact he looked as much the English gent as anything nearly seven feet tall can. He disentangled himself elegantly from the armchair, and enclosed my hand in his smooth, cold grip.

"Mr Eric Martell," he said, and smiled as if he was doing me a favour, saying my name. But he was really checking that he had got the right man. For Surks are careful never to make a mistake; the work they do, one mistake and they're dead. "Mr Eric Martell, the landscape painter?"

"The same – help yourself to more whisky when you're ready."

He nodded, gracefully. Surks are crazy about whisky; one sip and they can price your brand to the nearest penny. But they never show a sign of drunkenness. Something to do with their alien metabolism.

I waited, still fascinated by everything about him, though most people were pretty used to them by now, at least on telly. It was different when their ship first materialised out of the air over the parliament building in Stockholm. They chose the Swedes, they said, because in their opinion, the Swedes were likely to take their arrival most calmly. I must say, they did their best to play it cool themselves; their ship looked superficially like the biggest kind of civilian helicopter. They stayed inside it, but conversed through their quiet tannoy system with the local traffic-policeman. They spoke, of course, perfect Swedish. They even moved their ship when told they were interfering with traffic. The policeman thought they were students, playing a joke, until the first Surk emerged. Before he could panic, the Surk had allowed himself to be arrested, and handcuffed, on the charge, no doubt, of being seven feet tall and dark green in colour. Once inside the Stockholm police HQ, he was swiftly processed from the chief of police to the minister in charge of home security, and within an hour, was talking to the Swedish prime minister, and drinking surprising amounts of his whisky.

The prime minister asked whether he might invite along some scientists? The Surk produced from his briefcase several floppy discs that not only fitted the main Swedish government computer, but furnished every desirable fact about the Surks and their rather unimportant planet, unmentionable light years away. He also politely refused to be subjected to any unpleasant medical examination; he was a trader, not a botanical specimen. But he would speak with the ambassadors of Norway, Denmark, Holland, Switzerland and Israel. When Russia and America were mentioned, he said he thought it unwise, to begin with.

When they were gathered, he told them he wished to trade bars of platinum for live butterflies of every known species. He gave them each a bar of platinum worth a king's ransom, said he would return again in a week, and simply dematerialised.

As you will remember, two Surk ships rematerialised. One over the Gobi desert and one over the Mojave desert. It is said the Russians used nuclear warheads against theirs; and the Americans lasers. It disturbed the world's weather for months afterwards. But when both parties had done their worst, the ships were still there, still untouched, and stating quite categorically that they had no wish to harm or be harmed, nor to be imprisoned, dissected, brainwashed or any other indignity. They merely wished to trade bars of platinum for live butterflies. They would return in another three months.

It was quite a three months; a coup d'état in Russia, a new election in America, another revolution in Iran. Faced with a threat from space, the United Nations really became united. When the Surks returned, the businesslike Swedes had the butterflies ready, and received *incredible* amounts of platinum.

Five years later, the Surks returned to a chastened Earth, requesting a complete set of Buddhist religious statuary in return for a drug that could cure cancer.

When the deal was completed, the new Swedish prime minister, over a last whisky, commented that the Surks must lead a dangerous life.

"We are skilled in trading with violent primitive tribes," said the Surk. "It pays well."

Since then, their lives, on Earth at least, had got safer. Earth accepted it was a backwater, primitive but worthy of curiosity, like a late-discovered Amazonian tribe of head-hunters. The Surks wanted the strangest things, and it was obvious they worked for many masters stranger than themselves. But beyond that, they politely declined to answer. "Go and ask a Surk" became a rude saying in most Earth languages.

There are only two things you need to know when dealing with a Surk. Firstly, they are mercenaries, who will do any foul job for money, and secondly, they always tell the truth. If they make a bargain, they keep it. It's what they choose *not* to tell you that's worrying.

"Mr Martell," said my Surk, "I am offering you three weeks' work, and a voyage through space. This, we have not yet offered any artist. It is a new and potentially dangerous extension of our trading. Nevertheless, we undertake to return you safely, in good health of body."

"And mind?" I asked, sharply. He sighed, and put his

hands together, as if praying, like they do when they reach some point of difficulty.

"That is the snag. You will be alone for three weeks – the inhabitants of this planet are such as would disturb your peace of mind to see . . . I should visit you twice weekly to ensure your needs are met . . . you may take a domestic pet. . . ." He glanced at Vandyke, my black tomcat. " 'Vandyke will be of the company. . . .' " It was outfacing, that kind of remark. He knew my own trade and the culture of Earth better than I did.

"I've lived alone before," I said, a shade resentfully.

"But not in such strangeness . . . we will build you a house on this planet with grounds of your own choosing. We will build you Blenheim Palace, if you like. . . ."

I glanced around and said, stubbornly, "A replica of this house will do."

"And a large garden, full of Earth plants. . . ."

"What's the job?" I asked. The bluntness of Surks invites bluntness back.

"The people of this planet are . . . realists. They do not dream, they have no visions, they have no art. They want you to paint their planet, so they can understand what art is . . . You will come back a millionaire. . . ."

"Give me two days to think about it."

But I went. To Aramor.

The whole point about Aramor is that the hills are alive; and I don't mean with the sound of music. I mean, from little hills like the ones round Bridport, to the great distant snow-capped ranges like the Himalayas, you can see them *breathing*. They breathe slowly, less than a hundredth the speed of a human being, but they go up and down. They are rounded, like a woman lying asleep, and their green, grassy pelts are elastic, so there are no gaping fissures or sudden landslides. But everywhere you look, the surface of the planet is in constant motion. It is like standing on the deck of a ship

136

when a slow heavy smooth sea is running; at first, it makes you feel seasick, but you soon get your sea-legs, and the nausea passes. In time, you can walk, or even run, without difficulty.

And you breathe the same air the hills breathe.

Do not misunderstand me; it is not unpleasant. Each hill smells a little differently, each hill smells of itself. They smelt as different as a healthy dog smells from a healthy cat or a healthy horse. Or a healthy well-washed woman. The smells are nearly all pleasant, but they are animal smells, not the vegetable, mineral, chemical smells of our earth.

"You've given me some garden," I said to the Surk, who had deigned to tell me that his name (as near as any human could make the sound) was Astolid. "Must be ten acres."

"It is a replica of the gardens of your stately home of Tatton Park. That was designed by Capability Brown and Humphrey Rep-ton."

I felt a slight urge to kick him for his know-it-all, planned-it-all smugness. But all Surks are like that. I supposed you could get used to it in time.

"I don't like it," I said ungraciously. "I'm going to have to walk across it before I can even *see* anything of Aramor. I've got to live with the landscapes I paint. How'm I going to get the *feel* of the place?"

"You will get it soon enough." He gave the kind of slight knowing snigger they always give. "My worry is that you will get too much the feel of it. But I have done my best for you. You notice how still the ground is, here?"

I grunted; I had to admit the lawn I was standing on was a lot stiller than most of the hills I could see.

"We have put you on a dead hill."

"Why – is the planet dying?"

He shrugged. "No – like most things it is dying and getting born, every moment. Like the cells of your skin. Come, I will show you." He gestured towards the globular silver runabout we'd arrived in. We took off and hovered at five hundred feet.

The hill (on which my house and garden looked like a small pocket-handkerchief) was different from the rest. It looked like a sleeping woman or a stranded whale all right, but it wasn't breathing. And the glossy green hide of it was peeling away and falling downhill, in a series of earthy landslides. Bones of pale grey stone, or what looked like pale grey stone were showing through in sharp ridges. The old breathing cavities, that every hill had, were enlarged into crumbling black pits. It had an air of sadness, death and desolation. But the Surk pointed to where, on one death-grey flank, two new mounds of brilliant green, pulsating very fast like human breathing, were thrusting up through the elegant wreckage, like healthy pimples.

"Do not lapse into your earth morbidity, friend. Life returns."

Before I could think of any putting-down reply, he flew me back to the entrance hall of my house. My house, or the replica of it, looked a little absurd. Situated normally at the end of the main street of Bridport, it is, of course, a terraced house. Set here, it looked like a tooth snatched from its fellows. My neighbours' chimneys and wallpaper decorated my end walls. I allowed myself an inner smirk at the Surk's expense.

Immediately, my neighbour's wallpaper and chimneys vanished, to be replaced by honest, seemly grey stone. The Surk and I looked at each other, without words; there was no need of words.

"We are not liked by the Universe," said the Surk. "But the Universe pays us well. . . ." He shrugged, lifting his hands, palm up, in that slightly Gallic gesture.

"This house is too big," I said, narkily. "It's much bigger than my house."

"A little bigger," he said. "To hold the machinery."

"*What* machinery?"

"The machinery that will look after you. The house will

138

cook for you, clean itself for you, keep you as warm or cool as is best for you. Cure you if you get ill . . . we cannot afford to have you ill."

"Why can't *you* look after me?" I was growing unreasonable.

"You must not see too much of me. You came to paint this planet, not Surks. I will show you how to programme the house."

He opened a portion of hall panelling and showed me a control panel that certainly never saw the light of day in my own house in Bridport. "We want you to be as comfortable as you *can* be. Do you wish to live as if in the house of a houseproud woman? Who tidies away your magazine as soon as you put it down and leave the room? Or do you prefer to live with a slut, who will let your rooms be untidy and let your dishes pile up in the sink? You can make your choice on these buttons . . . press one for 'house-proud' and ten for 'slut', or anything in between."

He went on to show me other things. And then left. I think I half hated him; but I hated more to see him go.

I drifted around the bleak silence of that house. Silent because there was no traffic accelerating up Bridport's main street outside, no squeak of pramwheels or chattering old ladies, or deliverymen unloading their vans into the shops. It was quieter even than an early Sunday morning, because then at least there was the clink of milk bottles. Here there was only, where the distant sound of waves on Bridport's shore might have been, the faint sound of the breathing hills. I was about to break out in a sweat of pure unbelieving terror, at the utter silence, when there came an indignant miaow from what must be my studio.

And there was Vandyke, outraged at his captivity, clawing viciously at the bars of his alloy space-receptacle. I confess I lifted him out and hugged him. The smell of the studio did me good, too; the stink of turpentine, paraffin in the old galvanised bucket, drying linseed oil, and varnish. Sharp, fierce, chemical, blotting out the bland animal smells of this world.

Vandyke and I explored together. I must admit that the Surk had done well. *Everything* seemed in its place, the slow tick of the grandfather clock in the hall, the dying daffodils in their vase of green water. But Vandyke seemed dubious. He sniffed every single thing, clawed the carpet and the curtains, and left his strong-smelling trademark shared out sparingly over half the house. (He is a full tom; I have my freedom, he has his.) I didn't check him, or clout him, as I would usually have done. I felt the more of Vandyke I had, the better. Vandyke was all I had of Mother Earth.

I poured myself a stiff whisky, took up a week-old copy of *The Times* and tried to settle in my study.

I couldn't. I prowled again.

When I came back, *The Times* was back in the newspaper rack, and the glass had been put back on the sideboard. Washed and dried. . . .

I remembered I had left the housekeeping panel on 'houseproud'. It should have been scarey; but in fact it braced me; it was something to fight against.

I suppose the next half hour was a kind of frenzy. At first I did mild things, like leaving another half-empty whisky glass and paper on the table, going out, and then as suddenly returning. But already the paper was gone, and the glass replaced and dry. I ended up in an orgy of wrecking; smashing glasses, hurling one though my favourite window. Throwing the furniture about. Smearing a bottle of tomato ketchup all over the hearthrug. Then I left, meaning to return in ten seconds, and catch the machinery at it.

But of course, the machinery simply locked me out. After two minutes of alternately trying to kick down the door and listening for furtive movements inside, the handle was released and I came back to a perfectly tidy room.

I sat down, breathing hard, and got some kind of grip on myself. Then I noticed my old black telephone. Snatched it up, got a dialling tone, and dialled my best woman-friend. I don't know what I was expecting. A tape-recording of her? My voice relayed back to her home on earth, through countless million miles of space? I wasn't really rational.

Of course, I got the Surk. Not very pleased with me.

"You are sending yourself to the fringe of a nervous breakdown," he said accusingly. "If you go mad, I lose all my commission, and you don't get a penny. Why don't you settle down and do some painting? There are tranquillisers in the medicine chest in your bathroom. . . ."

"I feel *lonely*," I roared.

"You told me you'd spent three months on your own. All I am asking you for is three weeks."

"But then I was lonely from *choice*."

"You chose the million pounds."

"I want to hear somebody moving about outside," I bleated. "I want to hear somebody breathing besides myself. And those bloody hills."

"I suppose you're saying you need a woman. . . ." He sounded as tarnished as a Port Said pimp offering you his sister, young schoolteacher, very clean, very cheap. "All right – it can be arranged – it will take time, that's all. I'll come over straight away." He sounded almost weary, for a Surk. And when I met him at the front door, he looked a little disarranged, for a Surk. And he smelt so strongly of whisky, I actually apologised for bothering him.

"It does not matter," he said. "You'd better look at these pictures and make your choice." He threw down what seemed to be a large leather-bound album, with incised gold lettering.

I sat down and opened it, feeling better now he was here.

The album was full of photographs of naked women. Quite the most stunning collection of women I had ever seen in my life, and, being an artist, I've seen a few. And they were all the better because there wasn't a trace of pornography. No falsely suggestive smiles or gaping thighs, but posed with

141

great dignity and grave charm. The way you might photograph your own beloved wife, if you had one, and went in for that kind of thing.

You must believe that I went through them with a kind of growing reverence; after all, I am a painter, even if mainly of landscapes. There were girls who would have kept Gauguin off the bottle for a month, girls who would have made Renoir weep with joy, or Modigliani want to live for ever. I was silent a long time, then I closed the book and asked, awed, "Who are they?"

"Robots," said the Surk, with a shrug. "Walking, talking, breathing, loving robots. Ideal human types, analysed by computer. Take your pick, and we'll make her for you."

It disgusted me. I threw the book at him. "When I want a bloody Japanese blow-up doll, I'll ask for one."

"Why don't you inspect the goods, before you turn them down?" he sneered. "We might surprise you. Besides, I want some sleep. I don't want you ringing me up demented half the night. Take your pick. I haven't got all day, these things take some making."

It took me ages, while he sighed and walked up and down with his sinuous lizard grace, and helped himself to my, or his own, whisky. In the end, I narrowed it down to two, and there I stuck. One did not surprise me; I suppose she was the ideal type for most European men. Tall and athletic, with long straight ash-blond hair. Widish shoulders, widish flat hips, long legs and a neat but not gaudy bosom that would not stop her playing a good game of tennis. Very large, frank blue eyes. A cliché; but *what* a cliché!

The other surprised me. Smaller, rounder, very much darker, with raven-black hair. She seemed . . . vulnerable. Her bosom was magnificent, if not a bit too large; she held one forearm half across it, almost defensively. But it was the hugeness of her eyes. Dark, vulnerable eyes.

You could say I said "yes" to the first; but I could not bear to reject the second. No point to explaining *that* to the Surk.

"Her . . . or her. Can't make my mind up," I said unreasonably.

"Make up your mind when you see them in the flesh . . . or plastic." He gave his unpleasant giggle again, and whipped out a slim communicator from his elegant tweed pocket. He dialled some numbers, glancing from one page of the book to the other, whistling through his over-long teeth. Then closed the book, said, "Expect me early tomorrow," and was gone, leaving me alone again.

But somehow he had eased me, enough to make a quick oil sketch of the sunset. (It gets dark quickly on Aramor, the day is shorter.) It was quite a sunset; the clouds do not blow across the sky as they do on Earth. The living hills breathe them upwards, so they look like the rainbow smoke of sweet-smelling chimneys. I was reasonably pleased with it when I'd finished.

It was the only thing I *was* pleased with that night. I went to bed, but not to sleep. I had thought the land my house stood on was still, till I lay down. But as soon as I closed my eyes, I could feel the movement. My hill wasn't breathing, which perhaps I could have got used to, like going to sleep on a ship. My hill was dead, but being pushed around by the living hills surrounding it, as they grew and prospered at my dead hill's expense. The movement came as a series of unrelated lurches and tremors. As in a building that was going to collapse. I lay, screwed up as tense as hell, waiting for the next lurch or tremor, wondering which direction it would come from. It was like trying to sleep with a dripping tap, waiting for the next drip. But worse was the smell coming in through the open windows. Animal, warm, disturbing.

I think I must have reached out and stroked Vandyke a hundred times in the dark. It would always start his savage, querulous ripping purr; that was all that kept me from running out screaming.

I slept at last, after I had drunk enough whisky. And

dreamt of Claudine, which I hadn't done for twenty years. I had met Claudine on the boat-train, when I was a very young man. A tall, thin, long-haired French girl, going home to Paris from a strict convent school, and keen in an innocent way to make up for lost time. On the cross-channel ferry we snogged out the voyage, wrapped as tightly as a parcel under the shadow of one of the lifeboats, with the odd burst of spray breaking over us. We continued our enthusiastic, harmless, innocent passion on the long hard dusty seat of a French railway-carriage. I only had two phrases, *Je t'aime* and *Je t'adore*, which sounded absurdly, even to myself, like "Shut t'door". She had no English at all that I remember. She took me to the buffet of the Gare St Lazare, and bought me my first coffee and croissants and we ate them, with long warm loving glances. Until she noticed the time, half past nine. She uttered one word, *Maman*; the light died in her eyes, she shook hands as formally as a *chargé d'affaires* and left me sitting there, like a fool, not even knowing her surname. I knew there was no arguing; the boat-train was one thing, *Maman* another. For three years I dreamed of her kindly, then forgot her. Well, that night I dreamed of her, and was only awakened by the sound of the Surk's silver runabout.

Filthy, unshaven, shaky-handed, I watched from my bedroom window as he descended on to my lawn, where the shadows of the trees lay long on the silvered dew. And then a tall blonde girl stepped out gracefully after him, followed by a smaller, darker one.

Both were stark naked. As they stood obediently, almost to attention like soldiers, side by side on the grass, the wind blew their long hair across their breasts. Full of excited disbelief, I pulled on my old green tartan dressing gown and hurried down.

"Well," said the Surk. "Hurry up and choose. I have more important things to do."

I glanced at their naked figures, then up at their eyes,

144

duckingly, shyly. Aware of my tousled hair and stubble of beard. But they kept their eyes firmly on the distant hills, like soldiers on parade. Timidly, I put out a hand and touched the blonde one's shoulder. I think I was hoping for the feel of plastic, synthetic. It would have told me where I was.

But her flesh was smooth and warm, with that soft elasticity of human flesh. Gently, I pressed deeper. Felt, beneath the skin, the start of the deltoid muscle, the bone of the humerus. As the wind blew, a little gooseflesh started up under my fingers. And I could see the faint blue ghosts of veins, under the whiteness of the skin.

It was a living girl. I watched her breasts lift as she breathed; her nipples stiffened against the chill of the breeze.

I snatched my hand away, in a sudden sweat of guilt, and said to her, "Sorry; I do beg your pardon!" I think I even blushed.

But her marvellous blue eyes continued to watch the horizon without expression. The Surk sniggered.

"You can't deny the quality, Martell. Look, they even *bruise*." His over-large, over-sinewy green hand grasped cruelly where I had gently probed. When it let go, there was a row of flaring red fingerprints on that white shoulder, that slowly turned to the blue of bruises.

"They'll even bleed." His long fingernails drove in on the same spot. Red crescents formed; a trickle of blood ran down the peerless white arm.

But the peerless blue eyes kept on expressionlessly staring at the horizon. If they had not, if she'd cried out or even winced, I'd have hit him. As it was, I said roughly, "Ey, watch it. She's *my* property."

"Don't fret – she's programmed to repair herself." And as I watched, the bruises, the crescent-shaped wounds faded, leaving only the thin trickle of blood, which dried brown and became only a dirty mark. None the less, I pulled a handkerchief out of my dressing-gown pocket, spat on it, and wiped away the stain. Till she was perfect again.

The Surk laughed. "Stop treating her like a new car . . . you going to start polishing her? I didn't think that was what you had in mind." He handed me a slim control box with ten buttons. "You can programme her from nymphomaniac to shrinking virgin . . . whatever turns you on. Or you can keep her in a glass case and dust her every morning. You can even programme her so that her bruises last, if you're into that sort of thing."

"You disgust me," I said, and meant it.

"What am I offering you, except the freedom of the city? Beat her up or polish her – it's up to you. Anyway, that's the one you want, I take it?"

I turned to the dark one. "Have they got names?"

The dark one turned her head and looked at me. "My name is Sushita. What do you wish me to do?"

I leapt back a yard. "What the hell's the game, Surk? They're human – you've drugged them. He's drugged you, hasn't he, Sushita?"

She looked at me, sadly, meltingly. "No. I am a robot. I am here to serve you."

I looked from her to the grinning Surk, and back.

"Open your mouth," I said. I peered in; perfect white human teeth, soft pink tongue, the uvula at the back of the throat. I poked my finger in, and touched it. She retched, broke into a fit of coughing that made her small round smooth back heave.

"Sorry," I stammered.

Again, the Surk laughed. "All her other orifices are equally convincing. You won't find a fault."

"She's human," I shouted. "*Human!*"

"I haven't got all day," said the Surk, "to stand here arguing." He picked up a spade that was leaning against the wall. *My* old worn garden spade, with twenty years of use and shine on the handle. "Stand back!"

I stood back instinctively. He raised the spade like an axe, and struck at her rib-cage with all his strength.

146

When I opened my eyes, she lay on the lawn like a rag doll, nearly cut in half. As I opened my mouth to scream, as I gathered myself to try to kill him, he looked up from where he was bending over her, and pointed a green finger inside the cavity on her rib-cage.

The glint of silver metal was unmistakable. The inhuman shape of a cylinder, with wires spreading from it in a silver web.

I still felt sick. As sick as if someone had broken a Ming vase or taken a razor to a Rembrandt.

"She was *mine*," said the Surk sarcastically. "Is it not lawful for me to do as I wish with mine own?"

Even though I'm not a Christian, I still felt like hitting him.

"Enjoy the one you chose," he said. He pulled another thin control box out of his pocket, and threw it down by the wreck that had been Sushita. Then walked off to his silver runabout.

"Don't bother tidying up, will you?" I shouted. "Do I have to live with that mess for the rest of my time here?"

He turned his head as he climbed in. "I told you – they're programmed to repair themselves. Then she'll walk to the depot and hand herself in for recycling."

I did not bother to watch him fly away. Instead, I squatted by the wreck that had been Sushita.

Her closed eyelids, tender as butterfly wings. . . .

Her eyes opened, and looked out at me sadly and meltingly as ever. "I am here to serve you. . . ." I drank in her face's still unspoiled beauty; there was a little mottled bruise, where her cheek had hit the gravel of my path. "My locomotor centres are damaged; I will renew in fifty-five minutes, forty seconds."

"Are you in pain?"

"What is pain?"

Yet she was shivering; the gooseflesh forming and departing like clouds across her dusky skin.

I suddenly wanted to draw, to draw what the Surk had done, the terrible contrast of soft flesh and silver wire; I

147

wanted to capture her beauty before she was recycled for ever. I straightened.

The other robot was standing behind me, still staring at the horizon, though her empty eyes met mine as I turned to her.

"Fetch my drawing pad, will you, please? And a 2B pencil?"

She went immediately. It wasn't until she was moving away that I realised she was shivering too.

For the first time on Aramor, I drew like I meant it.

My drawing lay on the gravel finished: it was good, I'd got what I wanted. The blonde robot waited till I had finished looking at it, then picked it up and closed the pad, tucking it under her peerless arm. And the pencil. But still I lingered over Sushita, as if she was the victim of a traffic accident. The life seemed to have withdrawn from her. Her eyes remained shut, her skin looked dusty, withered.

"Will she repair?" I asked, anxiously. "You sure?"

"In two minutes, thirty-seven seconds. Stand well back please; there will be radiations harmful to you."

"Why should you care?" I asked it curiously, not rudely.

"We are programmed to care."

I stood back.

"Stand behind me, please! Close your eyes!"

I was still obeying her when there was a godawful flash. When I looked again, Sushita was getting to her feet. I rushed across; there wasn't even a bruise or gravel mark on her, though I dusted off a few leaves.

Then she stooped and picked up her programming box, and began to walk away towards the borders of my estate.

"I don't want her to go," I said.

"You wish me to go, instead?" The blonde robot took her own programming box from my hand.

"I don't want either of you to go."

"That is not permitted."

"We'll see." I snatched the box back from her. "Go into the house!" She went obediently. I hurried after Sushita, but I

148

was slow to overtake her. She was striding to her destruction briskly, but it wasn't that. The view of her back was so heartbreakingly beautiful. The subtle hint of rib, under the silken sway of her muscles, the twin dimples in her hips, the tightening of her elegant calves, her long slim toes, glistening with the dew of my grass. They *couldn't* recycle her . . . she'd just been made . . . what a waste.

"Sushita!" She turned her magnificent eyes on me, but didn't falter in her stride. "Sushita. I do not wish you to go. I wish you to stay."

"You chose Neone to stay." It was said without accusation, without anything.

"I want you both."

"That is not possible."

"You will *stay*." I tried to grab the slender control box from her hand. Given her build, it should have been easy.

It was like trying to tear the gun-barrel from a tank. We struggled on across the park. I grew vicious, trying to break her hold; went for her little finger. I might as well have gone for a six-inch bolt. She was towing me along.

I fell back. I'm a strong bloke; played a lot of rugby in my time. I ran at her, putting in the most savage tackle I knew. I knocked her flat on her face, locking my arms around her, feeling the softness. Desire stirred. . . .

For a second. Then she threw me off. It was like embracing the metal arms of a combine harvester. Next second, leaving me so winded I could hardly breathe, she got up lightly, gracefully, and went on walking.

I caught up, hobbling, limping. Again she turned her melting eyes on me. "I regret causing you injury."

I grabbed one of her ankles. And was immediately pulled on to my face. I hung on, letting her drag me along. I managed to slow her up a bit; but I was dragged along as if behind a bolting horse. It grew painful, and I let go.

She went on walking. She was nearly up to my park gates. I somehow knew that if once she passed through them, she was lost to me.

"Stop!" I shouted. "I choose you. Neone must go."

She stopped, came back to where I was lying, helped me gently to my feet, then stood passive, obedient. I'd managed to bruise her breasts and hip, but already the bruises were fading. There was a solitary leaf in her blue-black hair. She handed me her control box submissively. Again I stood lost in the wonder of her.

Soft footsteps on the grass. I looked up, startled, and there was Neone heading for the gate, even swifter than Sushita had done. She too had her control box in her hand; she must have picked it up from the grass, where I'd dropped it in my struggles with Sushita. I despaired . . . then a thought came.

"Run to the house as fast as you can," I yelled to Sushita. She set off at a fantastic pace. She'd have won the Olympic 100 metres back home . . . the *men's* Olympic 100 metres. . . .

I followed Neone to the gate. As she raised her foot to pass through, I said, "Stop. I have chosen you. Run back to the house as fast as you can."

Obediently, she turned and ran. She would have left Sushita standing. Sushita, of course, turned and began to *walk* back towards the gate.

So I played it, for half an hour. Using the difference in speed between their running and their walking, I got them both back to the house.

My phone was ringing in the hall. It could only be the Surk. It was. Very cross.

"What the hell are you doing, Martell? You flipped your lid?" (Surks have an appalling taste for out-of-date slang.)

"I want to keep them both."

"No can do!"

"No can paint, then!" I shouted.

"No million pounds then!"

"You can stuff your Surkish million pounds up your Surkish ass!"

"You're insane."

"Yeah, insane."

"I gotta think."

"Just keep the girls stationary while you're doing your thinking."

I glanced through the open door, across my park. Halfway to the gate, Sushita stood, motionless as a statue. Across the hall from me, Neone stood equally still. She wasn't even blinking, or breathing. I gave her a gentle, tentative poke. Slowly, like a statue, she fell over. Lay, with one leg rigidly and absurdly in the air, like a shop window dummy.

I never felt so lonely in my life.

The only thing that happened, for the rest of the day, was that some time in the afternoon, a gust of wind blew Sushita over to lie in similar absurdity. Why the hell was the Surk taking so long to make up his mind? In the end, I drank myself to sleep.

"We are both here," said a soft voice. I blinked awake. There they stood, the pearly dawn light stroking their soft skins.

Had I detected a hint of approval in that voice? Approval that I'd put one over the Surk? I put the thought rapidly from me. Robots don't have emotions. That way madness lies.

"We would advise you to take a shower," said Neone. "The pores of your skin are getting clogged; the number of harmful bacteria in them is increasing."

"That bed is too rumpled for comfortable sleep," said Sushita. "If you get up, I will make it." They surveyed me calmly, dispassionately. In blue dresses, they might have been hospital nurses. I looked where they were looking; at my body. I'd pushed back my bedclothes for the heat, and my pyjamas were in their usual state of unbuttoned disarray. The slight paunch, that in waking hours I convince myself I haven't got, looked like a fat white maggot, with black hairs running down the middle of it. I hadn't shaved for two days; my muscles were clogged with whisky.

"You are ten pounds overweight," said Neone.

"Your intake of alcohol has suddenly become excessive," said Sushita.

"Nonetheless, your general bodily condition is satisfactory. A fortnight's diet and exercise . . ."

"Get out of my bedroom," I shouted. "And don't come back until you're asked. And knock in future."

"I will return to make your bed later," said Sushita.

"You must stay healthy or you cannot work," said Neone. They closed the door softly behind them.

Over breakfast they began to get on my nerves. They just stood, watching me obediently.

I indicated two chairs. "Won't you join me?"

"How can we join you?" asked Neone. "You are not broken in half."

"Sit *down*!" I said. They sat, one on each side of me, watching every movement of my lips, my knife, my fork. With the dispassionate curiosity of cats.

"Going to be a nice day," I said.

Neone gave me a careful account of the weather we could expect for the next week.

"You are displeased with us," said Sushita. "How can we improve ourselves?"

I thought of how they'd be at breakfast as Earth girls. Gassing, leafing through magazines, asking each other if this would suit them, or that. Smoking fags, painting fingernails, pouring themselves another coffee. Enjoying life. Ignoring me.

"You don't talk to each other."

"What is there to say? We share the same memory-bank."

"Help yourself to coffee . . . I mean *drink* coffee."

They got up, fetched cups, poured themselves coffee and sipped it at regular intervals, like metronomes.

"Now you are *more* displeased with us," said Neone.

"It's about time you got some clothes on," I snapped.

"Why? Are we not pleasing to you? Clothes would impair our efficiency."

"Look – your lack of clothes impairs *my* efficiency. I'm supposed to be painting landscapes. But all I can look at is *you*."

I took them to my bedroom, which has two huge old wardrobes. One, as on Earth, was full of my clothes; the other was full of my dead wife's; I hadn't had the heart to face them since she'd died. Not that I'd entirely lacked female company since. And when they went, they always seemed to leave stuff behind, which I bunged in the wardrobe with my wife's, without ever actually looking inside.

I looked inside now. Not that there was much point in looking on Neone's behalf; neither wife nor girlfriends had ever been five feet ten. Instead, I got her a pair of black jeans that had got too tight in the waist for me, and one of my blue check shirts. She hadn't been programmed to dress, of course. Trust the Surk not to waste effort! I had to dress her like a doll, or a little child. Put one leg out, hold your arm out . . . she did so, automatically, like my daughter Susan used to, before she grew up, and married a Canadian farmer.

"Stand up, Neone!" She looked pretty good, fresh and boyish. I even found her a broad leather belt, and a pair of matching leather sandals. I was so pleased with her, I gave her a light slap on the backside, as I used to give Susan, and said, "Go for a walk and get used to them." As she went, I felt a rush of homely affection. I had made this mad world of Aramor a little saner.

I turned to look out some stuff for Sushita. And immediately it was different. Maybe it was just that Neone was gone; that I was alone in my bedroom with Sushita. Or maybe Sushita was different. Neone had lively candid blue eyes, that tempted me to make her laugh, or make her a little cross with me. Almost boy's eyes. Sushita's were like dark pools, fearful, yet expectant.

She is a *robot*, I told myself. She is the Surk's creature; he knows everything she does . . . the thought was remarkably

153

antaphrodisiac. I judged her height and weight, and plunged among my wife's old things; deliberately chose a countyish check shirt and prim twinset.

"Sit down, Sushita!" She sat on the bed, like Neone. Only it was not like Neone. She was trembling. I knew why the Surk had chosen her to attack with the shovel. And I hated the Surk for it, and hated myself.

"Put your legs out, Sushita! Put your arms up, Sushita!" And that wasn't the same, either. I had to break off, when I had got the sweater on to her, and go and stare out of the window. Neone was strolling on the grass in front of the house, and Vandyke was amiably chasing round her.

I turned back to Sushita. Clothes were not so kind to her, she needed a bra, she looked a mess. And I cannot abide a mess. I groped through the undergarments drawer, found an old white bra that seemed big enough.

My fingers were too clumsy; I must have pulled too hard, so she fell against me, and we both fell on to the bed.

I wakened from deep sleep and deep warmth, groping blindly to find out where I was. I touched a warm body, and the body responded. And then I remembered she was a robot.

I leapt from bed like a scalded cat. Stood by the window and stared out, as if my life depended on it. The scene outside echoed how I felt inside. One of the rare, freak Aramorian storms had blown up, a storm of such violence that my poor park was being shattered. Leaves and branches lay everywhere on the sodden turf; the trees, what was left of them, were bending like grass. The rain was sweeping down in solid rods, and Vandyke was nowhere to be seen; probably crouched in the dark warm hole next to the Aga, if I knew my Vandyke.

But someone was out there in the tempest. A tall, slender figure in a check shirt and black jeans that glistened and had turned almost transparent on her graceful limbs. Neone, still

154

strolling, or trying to stroll, as I had ordered her, two, three, hours ago. I say "trying". As I watched, the wind blew her off her feet. She got up again, struggled on, then a falling branch struck her, felling her to the ground.

I threw up the window. "Neone! For God's sake, Neone!" But she didn't heed. Maybe her hearing was damaged; maybe the wind simply blew my voice away. The wind blew me back from the window against the bed. I looked down stupidly, and Sushita just lay there, tangled in torn, soaking curtain, smothered in wet leaves, rainsplashed herself. But, as if she lay in warmth and comfort, she raised her arms to me again, like the awful automated penny-in-the-slot thing she was.

I ran downstairs and opened the front door. It smashed back against the wall, like a mad thing flogging itself to death. I forced my way out against the wind, step by step, almost leaning against the ground, my feet slipping on the sodden grass. I got twenty yards out towards Neone, and then fell, and the wind began to roll me back. I tried clinging on to individual tufts of grass. And then it lessened enough, so I could look up. Neone, returning on her metronome path, had come across me and stopped. Her hair lashed around her head like a living thing; there was blood on her face and on her arm, below the rolled-up sleeve.

"How may I aid you?" she said, carefully. Or at least mouthed against the shriek of the wind.

"Get home, Neone!" Then something else hit us. I felt her crawling powerfully, dragging me along; then I passed out.

I came to, lying on the couch in my lounge.

Gentle hands were bathing my head.

"You must lie still," said Neone. "You have been hurt, a little. Do not worry." The hands stopped bathing, and something cool, a patch, was pressed on to my forehead.

I opened my eyes. "Are you all right?"

"I have self-repaired." Indeed she had; even her hair was

155

dry, shone as if new-washed. The shoulder of her now dry shirt was badly torn, but it was not unbecoming. (Why hadn't *that* self-repaired?)

"My house – the park. Is it ruined?"

"All is self-repaired." I staggered to my feet, and out of the lounge. The front door of an immaculate hall was open, sunlight streamed down on an unchanged park.

"Would you like a warm drink? Tea? Coffee? Chocolate?"

"If you'll join me."

She was learning fast; she did not ask this time if I was broken in half. She fetched the drinks, and sat beside me on the couch, at a maidenly distance. She even managed to sip her drink at irregular intervals, so she didn't look like a metronome.

When I crossed my legs, she said, "Why do you do that? It is bad for your circulation, it will increase your tendency to varicose veins."

"It's a thing people do."

Three minutes later, she discreetly crossed her own. It was companionable. I said, "You'd better go and change that shirt."

"What shirt would you wish me to wear?"

"Choose one you like."

"I have no likes. I will bring them all down and you must choose for me."

I dressed her in a red one, and she took the rest back. When she returned, she said, "Sushita is still lying on the bed." Quite neutrally.

"Let her bloody stay there," I said viciously.

Neone and I spent a very pleasant evening. The leg-crossing business seemed to have stimulated her robotic curiosity. Mainly about Earth women and their wearing of clothes. I was unable to remember whether hemlines were going up or down at that particular moment; but I fetched my wife's old make-up bag and taught her how to paint her nails.

156

In return, she told me the dimensions, the extreme tempera-
tures and the weather systems of the planet Aramor. I tried
questioning her about the disturbing appearance of the true
planet-dwellers, but she said her memory-banks were blank
on the matter. I showed her how to lay and light a fire in the
grate, and told her my preferences about food. How fond
I was of fried liver; which cereals I liked for breakfast.
She worked hard to make herself into a more satisfactory
wifely robot. I must confess I did not find the process
unpleasant.

When we said goodnight, I showed her to the spare
bedroom, then went to my own. I confess I had quite
forgotten about Sushita.

Sushita still lay sprawled on the bed, though the house had
repaired its curtains and cleared all the dead wet leaves off
her. As I went across to her she raised her arms, lovingly. A
little devil seized me then. I had worked hard all evening to
make Neone act less like a robot. Now I worked even harder
to make Sushita more like one. I stepped back; she lowered
her arms; I stepped forward; she raised them again. I found
the exact point I had to reach before her sensors made her
raise her arms. I stood on it, and swayed backwards and
forwards, making her raise and lower her arms like an
automaton. When I had reduced her to a fairground slot-
machine mannequin and disgusted myself enough, I went
and slept in my second spare bedroom.

In the morning, I was awakened by the phone downstairs.
I drifted down in no hurry; let the Surk wait!

"You finally made your mind up?" he said. "It's the blonde
you want to keep?" He sounded so relieved I got narky.

"No," I said. "I want them both. I'm keeping the dark one
to hit with the garden shovel, like you showed me."

"Do not waste your wit on me. I could do with the spare
parts from the dark one."

"Look," I shouted. "They're both mine. I can do what I like
with them."

157

"I hope you've got enough strength to keep painting, that's all," he said, nastily, and rang off.

"Your breakfast is ready," said Neone. "I hope bacon and sausage will be satisfactory."

"If you'll have some."

"I can drink, but not eat. Eating was something they did not equip me for."

"I'm glad they've got their limitations," I said.

"I can also pee," she said, proudly. "But I think Earth women do not pee in public?" I stared at her in horror, thinking of little girls' peeing dolls back home.

"That was a joke," she said.

I could have hugged her.

After breakfast, we went exploring. I opened up my garage, thinking I might like a drive around my estate. But there wasn't a car. In place of my vintage Morris Oxford, there was a little silver runabout like the Surk's.

"Can you fly it?" I asked Neone.

"I have seen the Surk fly one. Robots learn quickly."

"Yes," I said. I noticed that she had changed the colour of her nail-varnish.

"I will attempt to fly it, if you wish. But I will fly it alone first. I must keep you safe and healthy!"

I stood back. She emerged in a series of jerks, waved me even further away, from behind the windscreen, then suddenly shot a thousand feet vertically into the air. She flew around in wild circles that had my heart in my mouth. Three times I knew the thing was out of control, and wondered desperately if she could self-repair the effects of a total crash. But she got smoother as she went along, and finally made a perfect three-point landing and got out, opening the door for me formally.

"My lord, your carriage awaits." Then added, "That is also a joke."

I did hug her that time.

I ran to fetch my sketch pad, and we had a marvellous day. I got a lot of sketching done. There was just one snag; I saw a line of mountains afar off that seemed – different. Interfered with. I asked her to fly me over.

"*No*," she said. "That is where They live. You must not see them, standing all together. They would drive you insane, just to look at them. That is forbidden."

I glowered.

"Do not be angry and black. I will take your mind off it. Shall we go home fast? Fast and low?" We flew home at zero height, curling round the breathing hills and over dark lakes, in a way that terrified me, and I loved it. When I got too terrified, I watched her pale profile, and the sureness of her pale hands on the controls. She had a way of tightening her mouth for the difficult bits, that was unbelievable in a robot. I could have sworn she was enjoying herself. When we landed, I gave her a smacking kiss on her cheek.

"Is that a sign of approval for Earth women?" she asked.

"That was a joke?" I asked.

She actually smiled.

"What a clever little robot you are!" I said.

"I am glad you find my performance satisfactory."

I should never have looked in on Sushita before I went to bed. I should have been satisfied with being happy; it was wrong to want to gloat on top of that.

But she was nothing to gloat over. Her arms were raised in a loving gesture all right. But they did not move. Then I noticed she wasn't breathing. When I touched her, she was as stiff and cold as a statue. Her skin looked dusty, a little wrinkled perhaps. A small Aramorian spider had begun to spin a web between her outstretched hands.

I panicked. I ran for Neone. But she wasn't in her room; she wasn't in the house. I opened the front door and shouted, but she didn't come. I rang the Surk. No reply.

I ran back to Sushita. In a panic, but in a rage too. The Surk would not steal her from me like this. Or was I to blame? For leaving her so long in one place, repeating the same piece of programming over and over? Had I mistreated and broken her?

I tried squeezing her hands. Stroking her. She seemed to begin to come back to life. There was the sound of breathing; but such painful breathing, an agony to listen to. Like somebody dying. Her outstretched hands made little flexing gestures, as if she was pleading for help. Or was it just the defective machinery? Her eyes flicked open, and they seemed full of uncomprehending terror. It got more and more awful. Her face was twitching in agony. Or just mechanical failure? She was so *cold*. I lay on the bed and wrapped my arms around her, trying to warm her, so her machinery could work better. Her breathing grew quieter, her arms relaxed to her sides, her whole body grew a little warmer, softer.

But she was only half right, however close I held her, however hard I stroked. And she stared and stared, pleading. I sat up, baffled. What to do next?

There was only one thing I hadn't tried.

Would it work?

Slowly, slowly, it worked.

I did not know whether I loved or hated her. Whether I was giving her life, or punishing her for frightening me so much. And she, was she in ecstasy or agony? I couldn't tell. She was like Byzantium, rich, dark, and strange; raped by ignorant crusaders, or absorbing them into her dark immortal life?

She was a robot; but she had been programmed to feel, and those feelings were not mechanical. Some woman had once felt those feelings; somewhere, once, some woman had felt that programme. And in my loneliness I wanted to reach through that cold intricate technology, the mass of silver wires, and find *that* woman. Like a madness. . . .

I don't know where it might have ended. But some time after dawn the bedroom door opened. And there stood

160

Neone, in a crisp white shirt and a newly pressed pair of my blue jeans.

"Your breakfast is ready. I hope bacon and mushrooms will be satisfactory?"

I thought the cold rage I heard in her voice was my own mind playing tricks. But meekly, while she waited holding the door, I got dressed and went down for breakfast.

I didn't dare look at Sushita's face.

After that, I kept them strictly apart. Neone was with me by day and Sushita by night. Neone was never allowed upstairs and Sushita was never allowed downstairs. They agreed such instructions would not harm their mechanisms; I gave them permission to move as much as their self-servicing required. Each on their appropriate floor.

It brought peace and order. I discovered a tennis court (obviously a bit of Tatton Park by Humphrey Repton, since I'd never owned one), and dug out my old rackets from the cupboard under the stairs, and taught Neone tennis. It was a delight. She learnt quickly, as in everything. Not just the way to hold the racket, and the rules. I realised after a while that she was copying my strokes. She also, of course, copied my mistakes. So we had some hard tussles, which I managed to win while she still had something new to learn. I used to think of the old Surk, sitting monitoring my progress somewhere, quite baffled that I was wasting time teaching a sex-robot tennis. And afterwards, as the Aramorian sun set, and the shadows grew long across the perfect green of the court, we'd sit companionably side by side and sweat (they both had adequate sweating-mechanisms), and drink from a bottle of squash.

And then, being a clever robot, she began to spot the mistakes in my strokes, and try to tell me how to correct them. I told her quite sharply that I wasn't taking lessons from any blasted robot. So, instead, she corrected them in her own game, and began to win. I'd been no mean tennis player

161

in my youth, and could still hit the ball like a rocket, though I was slower around the court than I had been. And I knew a lot of sneaky tricks, like serving so that the ball fell just over the net. But one by one she learnt them all, and in the end, it was like hitting a ball against a brick wall. I lost 6-0, 6-0, 6-0, and flopped down on the old rotting bench in a rage.

She came and sat next to me, and looked at me with that curious being-on-your-side which all robots and computers have.

"You are exhausted. You are not very young. You will make yourself ill, if you go on."

"Yeah," I said, savagely. I noticed her artificial perspiration had made her shirt cling to her chest, and looked away. I did not wish to think of Neone like that.

"You can slow me down by using the control box – it is not just for sex, you know – it is for anything I am doing. You can make me timid and nervous."

"I'd sooner stop playing altogether."

"Very well. I shall miss our games."

"So shall I. But we can do something else."

"Yes," she said. She was very close; her eyes were clear and candid, and I could feel the heat of her, against my leg. I didn't blame her; sex was what she was built for. But that wasn't the way I wished to think of her. I reached for her control box, which was set on button five, average, and knocked her down to one. Immediately, she shuffled her bottom discreetly along the bench, until she was a couple of feet from me.

"I wonder if you'd like Earth music," I said. "Let's go and play some Beethoven."

Even that was not without tension. After I'd played her his second piano concerto, she said, "It is sad. He wishes to play like a child, but he is big and clumsy like a bear. He wishes to be joyful, but he gets angry. He is all locked up inside." Again she gave me that candid look, and I didn't think she was just talking about Beethoven.

162

But we still had good times; flying, especially flying low and fast; and climbing the great breathing hills. I told her a lot of old Earth jokes, so she could work on her sense of humour. Soon, she was telling new jokes, better than mine. I didn't mind that; all my jokes were second-hand anyway.

If Neone was my sunlight, Sushita was my darkness. Sushita saw my worst side; I experimented with her control box ruthlessly. If I was Doctor Jekyll with Neone, I was Mr Hyde with Sushita. I even set her at 'shrinking virgin' one night. She cowered back against the headboard of my bed, the sheets clutched up to cover her magnificent chest, eyes like pools of offered agony.

Magnificent, until I tried pulling the sheets away, and smelt the stink of fear, and felt the crawling shrinking of her flesh.

It killed desire stone dead. I learnt that night what a thin, bitter, cold world sadists inhabit, and I never ventured there again.

And on button ten she became – mechanical. Remembering the steely strength she had shown dragging me across the park, I knocked her down to three when I was tired, and only needed the warm illusion of her body wrapped round me while I slept. On three, she became almost maternal, and it was to her I muttered my fears and hates. She didn't say much, just listened and murmured softly. Till I remembered the Surk might be listening.

But we all had ten good days; I got a lot of painting done. The Surk turned up, demanding some results to show his masters, so it was just as well.

"Home, James," I said to Neone, getting back into the runabout and putting an arm along the back of her seat.

"Fast?" she asked.

"High," I said. It was one of those fabulous Aramorian pink sunsets, where the clouds sculpt themselves into hills

163

and canyons that mimic those of Earth, just ten times the size. Up and up we went, far out of sight of the ground. Just Neone and I, together. I was proud of her; I had taught her so much in the last ten days. I had taught her to be a lady. I could have passed her off at Ascot, Henley, Queen Charlotte's Ball, anywhere . . . a daughter to be proud of. I dallied with the idea of taking her back to Earth with me, in place of the million pounds. Wondered if the Surk and his masters would wear it.

When we came back below the clouds, the landscape was strange. We were nowhere near home.

"What . . .?"

"I have a surprise for you." She landed, still in the sunset.

I was enchanted. A narrow little rocky valley, down out of the wind. A small waterfall, falling over a cliff, into a deep pool with trees clustered round. It might have been Earth, except the trees were deep red, with leaves that stuck up vertically.

"I didn't know you had waterfalls on Aramor," I said, suspiciously.

"Very few. I thought it would be good for you to bathe. You have worked hard; you are hot and sticky. . . ."

"I haven't got any bathing trunks."

She giggled. "Who are you expecting to come along and be shocked at the sight of you? Shall I put my hands over my own eyes?" Her sense of humour was really remarkably developed, for a robot. Still, it says a lot for how I felt about her that I still insisted on keeping my underpants on.

The water was marvellous; like it is after a hot day on earth. Cool enough to refresh you, warm enough not to chill you. I splashed around like a boy, trying to remember a faint memory of having once done the same before. . . . Till I became aware that someone else was splashing around with me. Rather abruptly aware, since she ducked my head under, without warning.

So then I had to do the same to her. She let me, even

though I knew she could have torn me in half. Her body under water was like a slim seal's. I got out of the water soon after, and lay on the short red grass. She went to the runabout and fetched me a towel, and lay down beside me. Close. But what real harm in that? We were still panting and laughing. And yet my eyes kept being drawn by her skin, with the droplets still running their uneven way down it. Something made me touch her, and in a second her arms were around me, and we were pressed together.

"Stop!" I said. And it was an order. She froze, still looking at me.

"I do not wish you to be like that, Neone."

"But it is what I was made for. You have twisted me, making me fly and laugh and listen to music. That is not what I am for."

"I am sorry."

"Why have you made me into your daughter? Why have you made me act like a boy?"

"I . . . I . . . I don't know."

"In three days I shall go to the recycling plant. Having never been used for what I was made. Why do you give all of yourself to Sushita? Why does she get all of you?"

"I . . . I . . . respect you. I do not respect Sushita. I *use* Sushita . . . I am ashamed of the way I use Sushita."

"You use Sushita for what she was made for. It is *me* you abuse."

"I'm sorry."

"You admit you have abused me?"

"Yes."

"Then you must undo the damage you have done me."

"Yes."

"Why do you sound so ashamed? So reluctant? Am I ill-made?"

There was no possible answer. Except one.

It was the end of an innocence; afterwards, I felt black. Something was broken in *me*, now. Miserably, I got dressed

165

and picked up her control box, which had fallen out of my pocket. It was set on button eight, and I usually kept her on button four.

"Did *you* change that button?" I asked.

"How could I change my own button? Do you think I have free will, like you?"

We flew home in silence. I felt I had done some dreadful, irrevocable thing.

I had. As we landed, Sushita came out to meet us. Against my express orders. She was wearing my wife's old tennis-things and swinging a racket.

"I wish to be taught tennis," she said.

"Damn you," I said, viciously. "Damn both of you. Stand there and be statues. I never want anything to do with either of you, ever again."

Then I picked up Vandyke, who had come out to meet me, as greasy and smelly as ever. I carried him up to bed, and locked my door, and eventually, cursing all robots and thanking God I only had three days left on this blasted planet, I fell asleep.

I was slow to get out of bed the following morning, and listened hard before opening my door. The silence was slightly reassuring. I went down.

"Good morning!" I leapt a yard in the air. It was a stranger's voice, coming from my sunlit lounge. I poked my head round the door. A slender, leggy redhead with a fine Afro hairstyle and eyes beaming like green lamps was reclining on my couch. I knew she was leggy, because my wife's old green housecoat had fallen apart above the knee. And she was wearing nylons and high-heeled silver shoes, I seemed to remember.

She rose, pulling the housecoat together, as if she'd just noticed. Came across and shook my hand genteelly. "I'll get your breakfast. Will porridge and kippers do?"

"Who are *you*?" I asked, rudely.

"My name is Merlen. The Surk sent me as a replacement. The other one's upstairs . . ."

I ran upstairs to Sushita's room. A most elegantly naked black girl lay draped across my spare bed. "Hi!" she said. I didn't stop to hear more.

"Where's Neone?" I roared at the redhead. "Where's Sushita?"

"Out at the back by the dustbins," said Merlen. "They're being called for, this morning."

They had been dragged there, and not gently. They were grey and soggy with rain, and glassy-eyed. Somebody had tossed a pile of hedge clippings over Neone. One of her legs stuck up through the heap grotesquely. Somebody had emptied the contents of my kitchen waste bucket, teabags and broken eggshells over Sushita's dead face.

I ran back, berserk. The redhead greeted me smiling with, "Come and get your breakfast. It's getting cold." I sent her flying, with one push, into the grandfather clock, and grabbed the phone.

The Surk didn't answer. I ran back to Merlen, where she still lay entangled with the grandfather clock, still smiling bewitchingly.

"You in touch with the Surk? Well, tell him from me that if I don't have Neone and Sushita back in an hour, all hell's going to break loose."

"Would you please help me up?" she asked, politely.

"Get lost!" I shouted, rudely, and ran back to the dustbins. Began pulling the privet clippings off Neone, clearing them away from her face. But her face began coming away with the clippings, strips of soggy grey plastic stripping off what looked like a skull of stainless steel with wires. One of her eyes fell out, on the end of more wires; dull as a dead fish's. For Neone there was no return. I turned to Sushita without hope.

My phone was ringing; my eyes filled with tears of fury as I ran, so I kept falling over things.

"What the hell's going on, Martell?" I had never heard a Surk so thoroughly stripped of his charming veneer.

"You *bastard*," I yelled. "You unmentionable bastard. They're rotting."

"You said you wanted nothing to do with either of them, ever again. I've got evidence – I've got your voice on tape – wanna hear it, chum?"

"Look," I said, beyond reason. "I want them back *alive*. The same as they were. Within the hour. Or I'll . . . I'll . . ."

"You'll what, bub?"

"I'll build the biggest damn bonfire you've ever seen, and tell these two new *things* to jump on to it and sit there till they roast to hell."

He chuckled evilly. "Whatever turns you on. . . ."

"And you know what that bonfire will consist of? Every damned painting I've done on this planet. How much profit'll you get then, Surk?"

Alarm came into his voice; I'd hit the right button. "Now wait, Martell, be reasonable!"

"One hour, I'll wait."

"You trying to start a civil war or something?" Then he gave a gasp, as if he wished he'd bitten off his tongue before he'd said that.

"What do you mean, a civil war?"

"Nothing, bub. Just my manner of speaking." But I could tell from his tone that he was both sweating and lying. "Look, be reasonable, Martell. These robots take time to build, even here. Take the strain till morning. Have a good time with those two new girls – a guy can do with a change of laundry every now and again. I'll have new models of Neone and Sushita to you before breakfast. Then you can keep the lot – start a harem!"

"I don't *want* a harem. Two is too many."

"You mean you only want Neone?" There was a glint of hope in his voice. Maybe he was having to pay for the new robots out of his own profits.

168

"I want them both!"

"Suit yourself." He rang off.

I heard the jangle of a grandfather clock being moved in the hall, and ran out. Merlen was pushing the clock off herself; pushing it upright from where she lay, with one elegant hand, reminding me again of the strength of these creatures. At the same time, her housecoat had somehow fallen open up to the second button, giving me a display of black stockings, suspenders . . . all the old-fashioned razzmatazz. Together with a very come-hither smile, like the worst of the porn-mags. Maybe she was an earlier cruder model.

"I'll have my breakfast now," I said coldly.

Immediately she rose, and was the perfect lady again. "I'll make some fresh coffee. It'll be cold."

I chewed my breakfast thoughtfully. Now I knew Neone and Sushita were coming back, I could be calm. Discrepancies were starting to stick in my mind like fish-hooks. If Sushita, when I first rejected her, had been walking back to the recycling plant, why were she and Neone now being allowed to lie by the dustbins and rot? And if the first two robots had appeared naked, why had the third appeared all togged up in my wife's old gear?

As if to compound my confusion further, Merlen, besides flashing the odd leg at me, was behaving much more like a human wife. She had actually lit up a cigarette, and was leafing through one of my old *Sunday Times* colour supplements, looking doubtless for the fashion pages.

At that point, the black robot arrived, wearing one of my wife's nightdresses and negligee, flung herself down elegantly in a dining chair, and announced she would die if she didn't have a cup of coffee. They kicked around the various fashion-pages together, ignoring me almost completely. Not acting like robots at all.

"Could I have another cup of coffee?" I asked, just from sheer bloody-mindedness; the pot was by my own elbow.

"Aw, help yourself, man; you're nearest," said the black robot, flicking the ash off her cigarette onto *my* floor.

I was suddenly seized with a doubt about whether they were robots at all. Where were their control boxes?

"Excuse me," I said, and ran up to the spare bedroom. The black robot's control box was lying on the bedside table. Marked clearly 'Charlene'. That set me wondering where Merlen's box was. It was on the bedside table in my bedroom. . . . I went downstairs carrying both, set at button one, for 'shrinking virgin'.

They were still both sitting, chatting about fashion. Perhaps disporting their limbs a little more discreetly. It suddenly struck me that they were being just how I'd wished Neone and Sushita to be, on that first morning when they'd sat drinking coffee like metronomes. They were learning fast . . . from each other? From Neone and Sushita's memory-banks?

"Fancy a game of tennis?" asked Merlen. "I'm a lousy player . . ."

"No," I said, "I'm going to have my evil way with Charlene here. C'mon, Charlene, up to the bedroom."

"Yes, *man*!" Charlene gave me a truly dazzling smile, and took my hand and positively hauled me up to the bedroom.

Two hours later, I staggered down dizzily, wondering how it would have been if I'd had her set on button ten.

"Lunch is served," said Merlen, rising with an equally dazzling smile. "Your favourite – roast duck."

"I haven't long had breakfast. . . ." I noticed she'd dressed herself more primly, in a black dress with a white Puritan collar. Only – too short.

"Let's not waste time," said Merlen ominously. "We've got to keep your strength up."

It was a day that went faster and faster. Lunch at half past eleven. followed by a repeated demand from Merlen that we play tennis. I played. Principally because Charlene had come down stark naked, and prowled around with her mind obviously on anything but tennis . . . at least when I was co-operating with one, it kept the other at bay.

Charlene served high tea at half past two in the afternoon. Afterwards she said I looked tired. I must not make myself ill . . . wouldn't I like to come and lie down . . . Instead, staggering with weariness, my eyes frequently closing, I painted her portrait. Quite a good one, in the circumstances, and some vanity seemed to keep her still. Till Merlen served supper at half past five. Back in her knee-gaping housecoat.

I rang the Surk. "These two new ones are getting out of control."

"Oh, go lock yourself in your bedroom, if you're scared . . . I'm busy." He seemed nearly as frantic as me, so I did.

I slept. Until nearly ten at night. At which point, Merlen broke down my bedroom door.

I was frank with her. I told her quite clearly that what I really needed was mothering. Looking after. Being protected from Charlene.

"Yes, yes," she said soothingly, pushing me back into bed. "Afterwards. . . ."

And, to be fair, she cuddled me with warm and peaceful affection, all night.

Afterwards, of course.

"Good morning," said Neone.

"Good morning," said Sushita. I peered at them through screwed-up eyes, in the dim sunlight that came through chinks in the curtains.

"What shall we do with Merlen?" asked Neone. Did I imagine a venomous keenness in her voice?

Merlen threw her arms round my neck, without opening her eyes. Warm, confiding, trusting . . . the very dream of an early morning wife.

"Shall we take her to the dustbin?" asked Sushita.

But Merlen had kept her word; she had cuddled me all night; afterwards.

171

"Let her stay. She can wear that black dress with a white apron. She serves meals very nicely."

There seemed to be a disappointed silence. Then Sushita said, "What shall we do with Charlene?"

"Let her stand still in the hall – she'll make a lovely statue."

"You are very kind," said Sushita, neutrally.

I was tough on Charlene till teatime; kept on going in and out and hanging my cap on her upraised hand. But she wasn't a statue; her huge warm living eyes haunted me and finally I released her. That made my house, big as it was, much too full of females. Females who watched me expectantly. Sushita haunted the upstairs landing, emerging from her bedroom the moment she heard my footstep. Merlen, based in the dining room and kitchen, offered endless supplies of food and drink with endlessly brilliant smiles. Obviously the old saying that the way to a man's heart is through his stomach was occupying most of her data-bank. Charlene, released, drifted from place to place, specialising in squeezing past me in the narrowest parts of the corridors. Neone strolled outside, flirting with Vandyke, who had obviously taken a big fancy to her.

Neone won; I went for a long walk with her. Leaving the house, we passed the dustbins. A hand, now reduced to a stainless steel claw in a mass of grey mush, still stuck out of the hedge clippings. That had been Neone; yet Neone was standing, warm, pink and breathtakingly beautiful, beside me. I stood looking at the decaying hand; she looked at it, too, with no more emotion than if it had been a garden trowel.

"Shall I take it home, to remember you by?" I said, bitterly.

"The Surk would not allow it."

"*Why* do they have to destroy you?"

"We will have no purpose, once you are gone."

"Don't you *mind*?"

"Why should we – we are robots."

"You were women once. You are a copy of a real woman. What happened to her – what did they do to her?"

"Why should you care?"

"If I had known her, I think I would have fallen in love with her. Except she was too young and beautiful – she'd never have looked at an old wreck like me."

"You are beautiful too, Martell."

I gave a short incredulous laugh, that was more like a snarl. "I'm forty-six, Neone. Grey hair, overweight . . . even twenty years ago nobody would have called *me* beautiful."

"A woman might. . . ."

"Let's *walk*," I said. I couldn't bear to look at her. I felt I was going mad. You *couldn't* fall in love with a robot.

"Tonight," I said, "I shall paint you all. And that's one painting they're not going to get. I shall take it back to Earth. I shall make you immortal."

She took my hand and squeezed it. I walked on with the tears running down my face.

So, for the last three days, I painted them. I never painted better. It was not merely a paid job, like some I do. It was not even just a pleasure, like so much of my painting is. It was a monument, a tombstone, an epitaph. Whatever I did not put down about them would be lost for ever. I painted in fear of that, and a fear of overdoing it. But I couldn't put a foot wrong; I painted with rage, I painted with grief, and for the only time in my life, grief and rage made me into a Rembrandt.

The first night, as I washed out my turpsy brushes, Sushita waited for me.

"No, Sushita. I'm tired – I'm worn out."

"*Please*," she said, then added, "I know you love Neone."

It was the only thing that could have got me into her bed. In her calm acceptance of defeat, I loved her more than Neone. But it was Neone I went for a walk with, in the morning.

The second night, it was Merlen who waited for me. But I shook my head.

"There isn't enough of me, Merlen. I can't love you all."

Charlene never even bothered to ask.

I stayed calm, till the painting was finished. And then we all just sat and looked at each other. Charlene had Vandyke perched contentedly on her naked black thighs, stroking him, and he was purring to high heaven.

They were my family. And (I glanced at my watch) in ten hours, the Surk would come and take them away to the recycling plant. And ship me back to Earth with a wad of a million pounds in my pocket. As if nothing at all had happened.

But something had happened. I'd painted them; I'd loved them; there was something of me in each of them now. Was that to go into the recycling plant too?

Suddenly I realised how much I hated the Surk, and his blasted money. Why should he have it all his own way? Surks weren't robots. Surks could bleed; Surks could die. There was an old shotgun in my cupboard upstairs. With shells; though I hadn't fired one for twenty years . . . I went and fetched it; broke the gun, peered down the shining barrels. There were a few pits of rust, but not many. . . . Nine shells left in the box.

"Do not hate the Surk," said Neone. "He is doing his job – for money – like you."

"We'll see," I said wildly. I had visions of barricading the doors.

"That is not your gun," said Sushita. "That is the Surk's gun. Your gun is back on the planet you came from."

"This house is not your house," said Neone. "Your house is back on Earth. . . ."

I had a sudden horrible vision of the Surk pressing a button, and me and Vandyke lying alone in a mass of grey mush, like the dead Neone's hand out by the dustbins. The

174

dustbins would also be the same grey mush. If Vandyke and I were on the top floor, we'd probably fall thirty feet and break our necks . . . I had a nasty vision of the Surk laughing, and shrugging, and pocketing my million quid for himself.

Something hard nudged my leg. My knife, in my trousers pocket. I pulled it out. An old French knife, which folded like a single-bladed English pocket knife. But the handle was wooden, and the blade was four inches long and pointed. I'd used it for thirty years to peel apples, trim brushes. But it would kill a Surk, at a pinch. I got it out, and opened it thoughtfully.

"He is stronger than you," said Neone. "He will take it off you."

"I'll burn all my damned paintings – except this one!"

"He came and took them away this afternoon," said Merlen. "While you were out for your walk."

I rushed into the next room. All my drawings and canvases were gone.

We set off at three a.m. I carried a torch, and the shotgun that could turn to mush in my hands at any moment; and my knife that wouldn't. Charlene carried Vandyke in his alloy space carrying case.

"We are all going to Heaven," she said neutrally, "and Vandyke is of the company." The other robots giggled; Neone's sense of humour seemed to have spread to all their memory-banks. Neone and Sushita carried food and drink; enormous bundles they had made for themselves and carried quite effortlessly. Merlen carried the first-aid kit from the bathroom, for my sake. We headed through the gates of my estate, under the strange, alien Aramorian stars.

I knew it was pointless; I knew they were only humouring me. But I would not sit and wait for the Surk to come for them.

I would make a protest; make it as hard for him as possible. I was going down into my dead hill.

175

It wasn't difficult to find a tunnel leading down, even in the dark. The huge curved flanges of rock stuck up everywhere through the slopes of dead soil. But I rejected the first two tunnels as being too small and narrow; it would not be amusing to be found by the Surk in the morning, stuck within fifty feet of the surface.

I found the biggest hole, under the biggest flange of rock, and started down.

"It is dangerous," said Neone. "It may all collapse at any time."

"You mean, this is one of the things the Surk can't renew? I'm very glad to hear it."

"You must not hate the Surk – he is only a paid servant."

"You'll be telling me next he's only carrying out orders – like the Gestapo."

"It is unwise to enter."

"To hell with it." I started down the steep slope digging my heels deep into the loose soil. The soil began to move under my feet, in the beginnings of a landslide. I grabbed for a flange of white rock, as it swept past. A large piece came away in my hand, and I was swept on, holding it, till I dropped it in disgust. It was crumbling between my fingers. It frightened me, how rotten the rock was. What was holding up the roof over my head?

But I had to keep running, keep ahead of the avalanche of soil and small stones that, coming from behind, was threatening to sweep me off my feet and engulf me. And the running into what I could never hope to climb out of exhilarated me, became a madness. Down and down I ran, the light of my bobbing torch sweeping wildly over great white roof-arches. I thought I might run down for ever, but it came to an end at last. The slope grew less steep; I slowed to a walk. The last ten yards I had to walk ploddingly, as the disturbed soil, arriving after me, threatened to bury me to my waist.

A last tinkle and rustle of soil, then silence. Total silence. I thought I must be at least a mile underground, alone.

I suddenly got frightened the Surk might take the robots, and just leave me here for ever . . . no, he had given his word to keep me safe . . . or was there something in the small print of his Surkish contract that stated that if I put myself in danger deliberately, he would be excused his obligations?

Panicking, I shouted for the girls. My voiced echoed and echoed into the blackness of a huge cavern. I shone my torch upwards; it was a very powerful torch, but only the very tip of its beam glanced across a row of gleaming white arches, narrow and close together. It was like being inside the greatest cathedral ever built. It was like being inside a human rib-cage. . . .

And my shout was not without effect. Far off, down the cavern, rock broke free from the ceiling and crashed to the floor; I remembered the chalky crumbling of the piece I'd held in my hand . . . had to stop myself whimpering . . .

A rushing, rumbling . . . behind me. But when I whirled with my torch, it was only the earth slope moving again, as Neone came leaping down it. She seemed to be grinning with the very glee of it, but as she staggered up to me, and I embraced her from sheer joy at the end of loneliness, she straightened her face and said, "You are a fool, Martell."

Then Sushita, coming much more slowly and carefully, not enjoying it at all, then Merlen, and finally Charlene with Vandyke. It was good to hear Vandyke's noisy complaints.

"What now?" said Neone. "What is the end of your foolishness going to be?"

"Since we're here, let's explore," I said, more light-heartedly than I felt.

So we explored; on tiptoe and in whispers, for fear of another roof-fall. I saw a lot of things I couldn't understand. At one point we came across a white boulder lying in the way, with huge wings of rock thrusting up from it. It must have been fifty feet high, and there was a round tunnel running through it, ten feet in diameter. It reminded me of something; it was only later I realised it looked like a massive human vertebrae.

It was soon after that that the thumping started. A rhythmic hollow thumping that was somehow familiar, comforting, reassuring. Instinctively, in the cold darkness, amidst the flicker of black crumbling soil and white rock under my torch beam, I made for it.

I thought I heard Sushita, behind, give a little 'yes' of approval, though it might only have been a sigh. Then Neone said, quite clearly, "Yes – but the point of greatest danger."

The thumping got louder, till it was all around us; sinuous swishings too, and the sound of wind blowing through galleries. It all made me feel, unreasonably, *safe*. A kind of rootless, illogical sense of safety and wellbeing that got stronger as I got nearer the sounds. But at the same time the girls closed up round me; Neone in front, Sushita and Merlen to either side, and Charlene still behind.

The very rock and soil beneath my feet was trembling now with the deafening thumping, and yet I pressed on, drawn by the noises that somehow meant total safety. As if I was enchanted, and couldn't stop.

There was a creaking sound ahead. I flicked up my torch and saw a curving white wall that extended all around us. A dome – we were inside a white dome half full of black soil – a dome as big as the dome of St Paul's.

And then, under the light of my torch, black lightning ran up the white wall of the dome.

The dome was cracking.

"Sit down," said Neone, sharply, urgently. I obeyed without thought. They thrust poor Vandyke in his carrying-case on to my knee, and all four leaned over me.

And the roof fell. . . .

When I came to myself, my torch was still shining. Vandyke and I were in a very narrow place, smaller than a two-man tent. And the sides of it were crumbling white chalky rock,

178

and all that was holding up the rock were the arched bodies of Neone, Sushita, Merlen and Charlene. I was in a living tent . . . or rather a robot tent.

"I am not seriously damaged," said Sushita.

"My arm is broken, but I can hold," said Merlen.

Charlene said nothing. Her eyes were shut, and her face grey.

"She will rebuild herself," said Neone, comforting me. Then, "Can you hold?" to the other robots. And then she began to dig away the white rock in front of her. Like a humanoid bulldozer, like a grab-shovel. I thanked God, then, for the power in my robots.

It took a long time; my breath grew shallower and shallower as the air began to give out. Every time Neone returned to us, she was more damaged; her hands were just steel skeleton-claws. I shuddered. She smiled, sweetly, robotically, at those hands.

"Not enough to make love with, Martell. But enough to dig with."

And then, just as Vandyke seemed to sink into a coma, and I despaired, a new flood of air broke into our space. Warm, animal-smelling life-giving air.

"Come quickly, Martell. We must not hurt the living hill more than we have to."

Somehow I crawled, hardly able to move with stiffness. And found, pushing aside a dripping warm curtain of what felt like flesh, that I was in a low rounded tunnel about three feet high. Pink, glistening under the light of my torch, soft, wet and full of sweet animal air.

I just sat with Vandyke on my knee and watched, glad to be alive. Neone dragged Charlene out next. Terribly gashed and eyes shut, but breathing and a good colour again. As I watched, her wounds began to close . . . Merlen and Sushita came together, still supporting each other like an arch, and the dead white stone collapsing after them. Our pink tunnel filled with dead white dust.

Next second, I was whirled away down the passage, wildly turning over and over, bouncing off india-rubber-like walls that did not hurt me. Explosions, again and again, whirling me on further and further . . . when they stopped at last, I was lying on my back in a much wider tunnel, still clutching Vandyke, and with the girls sprawled round me.

"What happened?" I croaked.

Merlen giggled. "The living hill sneezed; the dust of the dead hill made it sneeze . . . keep still, very still, Martell. Or you will make it sneeze again. . . ." Then all the girls were laughing; they were nearly whole again; even the rents in their clothes were mending themselves, though I had a cheering view of Charlene's left breast.

"This is good enough," said Neone. "Here, we wait till morning."

Once I knew I was safe, I slept like a child.

I wakened with a start; groped wildly for my torch in the blackness then, switching it on, looked at the time. Exactly ten a.m.

"Time for him to arrive," I said to myself; and reached for my useless shotgun and slid two shells into it.

"He is not coming," said Neone. Her voice came from above. I looked up, startled. They stood in a ring, pale and glistening in the torchlight, once again mother-naked and looking down at me. "He is not coming. We are taking you back." She reached over and took the shotgun from my limp fingers. Sushita and Merlen helped me to my feet. Their hands stayed on my arms; gently, but I could feel the strength in their metal tendons.

"Stop," I said. "Sit down."

"We no longer obey you," said Neone. "Your time is over."

I argued all the way to the surface; managed to grab one of their control boxes off them and punched buttons frantically. But it was quite useless. As we broke surface into a beautiful morning, I started to struggle. There was a silver runabout waiting; bigger than usual, but without a pilot.

I struggled so hard I began to hurt myself. Under Sushita's iron grip blood trickled down my wrist.

"I regret doing this," said Neone, and there was a sharp prick in my backside.

When I came to, the runabout had landed. In the middle of a huge arena that seemed to be made of pale blue concrete. Only, instead of seats there were tiers of boxes, rather like World War II pillboxes, with dark narrow horizontal slits for looking out of. I knew eyes were watching me from those slits; a hum as of a hive of bees came from them, and I knew a great crowd of Them were gathered, avid with excitement.

The runabout's doors slammed shut of themselves; in the humming silence they made a sound like gunshots.

The runabout took off silently by itself. It was like a last desperate hope being taken away.

"It is time," said Neone.

Across the arena were a pair of twin doors. Now they rolled back silently letting out a white light so blinding that I had to screw up my eyes.

"What is it?" I said, swallowing on a dry throat before I could speak.

"The recycling fire," said Merlen, dreamily.

"What does it *do*?" My voice cracked and squeaked.

"It will vapourise us into our constituent elements, which will be cooled and stored for future use. Charlene will go first."

And Charlene began to walk towards the white fire. I watched her, feeling the heat on my face and eyes. I followed the elegant, arrogant swing of her black buttocks, the tendons tightening and relaxing under the gentle flesh of her long legs. Then, without pausing, she walked in through the doors and into the fire. And melted like a plastic toy soldier. And was gone.

Even knowing she was only a robot, I felt very sick.

"Me next," said Merlen. She sketched me a slight salute to her forehead, smiled and went. And melted like Charlene.

"No, wait!" I said to Sushita. She turned, eyebrows uplifted, eyes full of what seemed great affection.

"Goodbye," I said. "God bless." Knowing I'd never said a more stupid thing in my life. She smiled, tilted her hand and walked. It seemed to me she lasted longer than the others; got deeper into the flames before she vanished. I thought I could have died then. Sushita had always been a loser; but the most loving loser I'd ever known. And she'd had something of me in her.

And then Neone was walking. I let her get ten yards then I sort of . . . snapped. I began to run after her, towards the flame. The heat was burning out my eyes, searing up my nose and down my throat. Then I seemed to hit a kind of wall of cool invisible glass. Even as I slid down it the glass was cool and pleasing to my hands.

Beyond it, she stopped and turned half back, and smiled at me. Then she too was in the flame. She seemed to last longest of all; turned back to wave to me, proudly. I thought for a crazy moment she was going to survive it. Then her body thinned to a black skeleton with rags of burning plastic falling off it, and she too was gone.

The doors shut; the cool glass screen vanished, landing me flat on my face.

I lay there, in the silence and sunlight. Aware of all the eyes in the dark slits, watching. Alone, except for an indignant miaow from Vandyke somewhere behind.

And as I lay, I heard a sound I knew, and glanced up in disbelief. A green Surkish spacecraft was taking off, beyond the next low ridge.

The Surk had gone without me.

I crawled back to Vandyke in his carrying-case; pulled out my puny knife.

"Damn you," I shouted at the slits. "Come on, then. COME ON!"

182

The humming rose to an even higher pitch of excitement. Then a door in one of the pillboxes began sliding back. Revealing only darkness.

I suppose I should have fainted then. Or run up and down screaming, my mind in tatters. But an odd bloody-minded bit of *homo sapiens* took charge. The Neanderthal bit, probably. It pointed out with low cunning that there was a flight of steps below that door; that any creature coming down steep steps is at a disadvantage if attacked; and that an upward thrust with a knife is a lot harder to parry than a downward thrust. *Homo sapiens*, simplified to brute killer, advanced with legs spaced well apart to the foot of those steps.

The humming changed its note; disapproval; disappointment. What did They expect, a pushover?

And then the creature emerged; and I dropped my knife, feeling like a stupid baboon squabbling over his bananas.

It was a woman; a very beautiful woman. Not young, maybe about fifty. Lines round the eyes and mouth. But the eyes were clear and luminous, the hair blowing like black silk, and the figure beneath the gauzy blue draperies might have been a girl's. She reminded me of the best of the American Blues singers; disciplined; a lot of pain and some bitterness; old as the hills in her expression, and yet she walked like a queen. And she wasn't a robot. Who would give a beautiful robot a hint of crepiness around the neck as it turned?

"You've decided defence is useless, Mr Martell? You can have your knife back if you like. Perhaps you'd feel more secure?"

I shook my head, stupidly. I felt about ten years old.

"The Surk said you were monsters. . . ."

"He did *not*. He said we were of such appearance as would disturb your peace of mind to see us." She allowed herself a wry smile, and gestured to the pillboxes.

Doors slid open everywhere, and women swarmed down

the blue steps, dressed in every colour of the rainbow. Some were little more than children, some whitehaired, but every one a stunner, walking like a queen. I could've fallen in love with every one of them, even the grandmothers.

"Where are your men?" I asked stupidly.

"No men," she said starkly. "They *would* fight. They came near to destroying us. And we had the power to have no more male children. We thought . . . as the men grew fewer, they would fight less. But they fought more. They killed each other off."

"Then you're . . . doomed."

"On the contrary, Mr Martell – we have ample . . . resources. Resources to last us several thousand years. In peace."

I glanced around at the women, who had formed a huge circle. I no longer felt inclined to fall in love with any of them. And certainly most of them showed little signs of falling in love with me. The mature ones, especially, showed a disapproval I hadn't seen since the headmistress of my primary school days, on the day we let the baby frogs loose from the fishtank. On the other hand, there were a scattering of twenty-year-olds who were surveying me with some interest. . . .

"Oh, well," I said huffily, "I hope the paintings were satisfactory . . ."

"You can take them with you when you go. We have our own art."

"Then what the bloody hell has all this cock-up been about?"

"Don't worry, Mr Martell – you will get your million pounds – it is already in your bank account on Earth."

"I am not *worried* about my million pounds. I want to know what all this cock-up's been about. I've been very upset . . . I . . . I . . ."

The older women murmured disapprovingly at my shouting. The younger ones looked even more interested.

184

"I suppose you are owed some explanation, Martell. Put it this way. Most of us are only too thankful to be rid of men. But the younger ones read of them in old books. The old books, being written by men of course, make men seem . . . exciting. It makes our young *restless* . . . they quarrel pointlessly . . . do silly dangerous things . . . sometimes get themselves killed. So we decided to settle their curiosity – to let them see men as they really are. We let the Surks bring us occasional men, as they brought you. On some pretext, like your painting."

"Thanks a lot," I said bitterly.

"I wish you would not interrupt. The men, of course, get restless without . . . sex. So the Surks provide them with sex-robots. . . ."

"Who are a lot more bloody fun than your women. I *liked* your robots. I only fell in love with one of your blasted robots, that's all. *Two* of your blasted robots."

I was on the verge of tears, and I felt like hitting her for it. Making me cry in front of a lot of long-faced women, who weren't missing a trick.

"You did not fall in love with robots, Martell. You fell in love, as you call it, with real women. We let our virgins live and feel through the robot bodies, so they can see what men are really like when they are without law, without restraint. When they have an endless supply of lovely female bodies to rape and torture and burn. When it gets too bad, we take the virgins' minds away and only the robots suffer. It cures most of our women of wanting men." She shuddered delicately.

"What do you do . . . to those men?"

"Send them home with the money we promised them. Why should we be their judges? They will destroy themselves in the end."

"And what about the men who don't rape and torture and burn?"

"You mean the men who only make the robots into whores and virgins, when they are neither? Why do you *always* have

185

to make women into whores or virgins, Martell? Why do you always dress them up like dolls, or teach them new tricks as if they were performing animals? You made Neone into your daughter, almost your son. Why could you not let her be herself?"

Again the circle of women murmured censoriously. I did not like the look of them. Except the young ones, who were giggling between themselves.

"But . . . What happened to *those* men?" I repeated.

"Such men, who are merely silly, and not vicious, we tend to keep. We lengthen their lives as long as possible, as we lengthen our own. Of course, the young women quarrel and bicker over them . . . but that is better than them doing dangerous things and getting themselves killed." She gestured to one side – towards a small group of men standing watching us, well back. Few were either young or beautiful. There were some bald heads, and some white hair, and one walked with the aid of two sticks. They nodded at me affably; they looked decent blokes.

"That all you've got?"

"That is all the tolerable ones, after thirty years of searching. . . ."

"And what about *me*?"

"You can stay if you wish. All four of the young fools would have you. Even Charlene, whom you used as a hat-rack. Perhaps she will make you stand for hours by *her* door, and hang *her* hat on *your* arm. She has a fine sense of humour, Charlene."

And there was Charlene, waving from the crowd, grinning from ear to ear.

"And young Merlen would have you – she would break down doors to get to you."

There was laughter from the women, but most of it was bitter. Merlen, further along, sketched her gay salute.

"Sushita . . . I would not let Sushita have you. She is too much in love with fear and pain." Sushita stared at me sadly,

186

from her place. The women murmured a third time, and a cloud seemed to cross the sun. I grew a little cold and afraid. But still a wild crazy hope was soaring inside me. Though their leader surveyed me sarcastically.

"Neone – I suppose you have brought great status to Neone. You tried to follow her into the fire. Our young fools will make a song about that – and put you both into some romantic legend." She nearly spat the last words out. "Myself, I would rather lie under the nareth trees with my friends, and drink tsassas. . . ."

I looked up, and Neone was walking towards me. Not a self-repairing sex-robot, but flesh and blood like me. If I made a mistake and hurt her now, I could not erase the damage with the press of a button. I grasped her hand to make sure she was real. The centre of her palm was sweating. She was trembling, like me.

"Can I keep Vandyke and my house?" I muttered.

Neone giggled and said, "I'll find room for it, in the corner of my palace gardens."

"What will the Surk tell them, back on Earth?"

"Some convincing lie. That is what Surks are paid for. Now I am taking you home, before *all* my friends want their portraits painted . . . in the nude."

The queen made a sound of profound disgust, and strode away down the steps.